AMMUNITION

Also by Ken Bruen

KEN BRUEN

AMMUNITION

 St. Martin's Minotaur ⚮ New York

AMMUNITION. Copyright © 2007 by Ken Bruen. All rights reserved. Printed in the United States of America. No part of this book may be used or reproduced in any manner whatsoever without written permission except in the case of brief quotations embodied in critical articles or reviews. For information, address St. Martin's Press, 175 Fifth Avenue, New York, N.Y. 10010.

www.minotaurbooks.com

Library of Congress Cataloging-in-Publication Data

Bruen, Ken.
    Ammunition / Ken Bruen.—1st ed.
        p. cm.
    ISBN-13: 978-0-312-34145-9
    ISBN-10: 0-312-34145-8
    1. Brant, Detective Sergeant (Fictitious character)—Fiction. 2. Roberts, Chief Inspector (Fictitious character)—Fiction. 3. Police—England—London—Fiction. 4. London (England)—Fiction. I. Title.

PR6052.R785A84 2007
823'.914—dc22

2007013590

First Edition: August 2007

10   9   8   7   6   5   4   3   2   1

FOR RANDALL HICKS

*I have never experienced institutionalised wrongdoing,
blindness, arrogance and prejudice on anything like the
scale accepted as routine in the Met.*
—Sir Robert Mark,
Metropolitan Police Commissioner

AMMUNITION

1

BRANT WAS ON his third whisky, knocking it back like a good un. He was feeling real bad, Ed McBain was dead, and nothing could ease the loss he felt. He muttered:

'Fuck.'

The barman, highly attentive to Brant's needs, asked:

'Yes?'

Brant gave him the granite eyes, said:

'I want something, you'll know.'

Brant's rep was legendary. In South-East London, he was feared by cops and villains alike. Numerous attempts had been made by the brass to get rid of him, but he had survived every effort.

London was in a state of high alert. Since the terrorist attacks, an air of paranoia ruled. It wasn't that the populace wondered if the bombers would strike again, but a question of where and when.

The only hero Brant had ever had was McBain, and he'd collected all the novels. He had the latest one. Alas, now the final one, and he couldn't bring himself to read it. He was about to shout another drink when he heard:

'Sergeant?'

He turned to see Porter Nash, the recently promoted Porter Nash, dressed in a very flash suit. Porter was the only openly gay cop on the squad and was probably their best investigator. Brant, who hated everyone, had an unlikely friendship with him. Neither of them could quite figure out why they enjoyed each other's company, but fuck, go figure, they just went with it. Brant said:

'Some suit.' Porter took the stool beside Brant, asked:

'You like it?'

Brant signalled for the barman, took a long look at the suit, said:

'It helps if you're gay.'

Porter laughed, most times it was the only way to go. You had dealings with Brant, you needed a great sense of humour or a sawn-off. Brant ordered two large whiskies and Porter protested:

'I wanted some vodka.'

Brant blew it off, said:

'With lime, I suppose. Have a real drink for once.'

The barman knew Brant, of course, everybody knew him, but the other geezer, he was new and very worrying. He had manners, said thank you when he plonked the drinks down, so he couldn't be a cop. But he had a look, despite the nancy suit, he had a way of holding himself, that was . . . not to be fucked with. The barman would keep an eye, see what he could discover.

Brant clinked his glass against Porter's, said:

'I think the bar guy fancies you.'

Porter took a quick glance, said:

'Not my type.'

Brant knocked back a lethal gulp, Porter sipped at his then, seeing Brant's expression, took a larger sip, said:

'Could I get some water for this?'

Brant was lighting a cig. He'd switched to a so-called low-tar brand, it wasn't doing it. Porter, six months without smoking, inhaled the smoke greedily, resigned himself to the neat whisky, asked:

'So what do you think of the Yank?'

Brant looked at his watch and, if he'd only known, he had maybe ten minutes before he was shot.

The *Yank* was L. M. Wallace, a terrorist expert. All the squads had been assigned one, the reasoning being that they knew when and where an attack might happen. As the Americans spoke of 9/11, the Brits, alas, now had 21/7. Brant stubbed out the cig, said:

'Haven't met him yet.'

His tone suggested he could give a fuck, but he asked:

'You met him?'

Porter nodded. He'd been assigned as mentor, guide, nanny, what the fuck ever, mainly to ensure the guy was made welcome. He said:

'He's big, I'll give him that.'

Brant laughed, his special filthy one that had no relation to humour, and he said:

'Hung, eh?'

Porter finished the drink and felt the warmth caress his stomach, the artificial ease. He'd take any relief he got, said:

'The guy is about fourteen stone and has a face that looks like someone blasted him with a blowtorch, and his credentials, impressive, I've got to admit.'

Nothing, nothing in the world impressed Brant. He asked:

'Impress me.'

The shooter entered the bar, the Browning Automatic in his jacket. He had racked the slide a moment before and was, so to speak, cocked. He saw the two cops at the bar. Got his stance in gear.

Porter said:

'FBI Anti-Terrorist Squad, Special Ops, Homeland Security, and a whole batch of citations.'

Brant digested this and was about to make a smart-ass reply.

The shooter had the Browning out. He was about to squeeze the trigger when a woman pushed open the door, knocking him slightly off balance. He muttered:

'Fuck.'

Tried to regain his balance, pulling on the trigger. Released a barrage of shots. Bottles exploded behind the counter, pieces of the counter flew in the air, and Porter pushed Brant to the floor, covering his body with his own. The gunman, seeing the cops down, hoped to fuck he'd hit something and legged it. People were screaming, a drunk, sozzled in the corner, came out of his stupor, asked:

'Is it Christmas?'

Porter was on his radio, screaming:

'Shooting, gunman heading from the King's Arms on the Kennington Road.' He stood up, the smell of cordite, mixed with the spilled booze, was heady. He looked down. Brant wasn't moving and Porter bent, put out his arm, saw the hole in Brant's back, he screamed:

'Get a fucking ambulance.'

To his radio, he shouted:

'Officer down, repeat, officer down.'

The drunk began to hum 'Jingle Bells.'

Ammunition. Powder, shot, shell, etc. Offensive missiles generally.
                    —dictionary definition

2

WHEN PC McDONALD heard Brant had been shot, he nearly punched the air, wanted to shout:

'Fucking brilliant.'

But he was in the police canteen and had to act like the others, pretend to be shocked, outraged, jumping to his feet, ready to seek out the shooter. He was shocked all right, couldn't believe that someone had finally got Brant. He hated that bastard with all his heart. There'd been a time, Jesus, how long ago? McDonald had been golden, the kid on the way up, earmarked by the Super as his boy. All he had to do, simple really, was ensure that Brant got fucked and good.

Piece of cake.

Alas, piece of very poisoned cake.

Brant was such a wild card, such a maverick, that all you had to do was watch him, let the proof fall into your lap, bingo, he was gone. But Brant got wind of it, and ever since, McDonald's career was in the toilet. Fuckup followed fuckup and always, behind each new disaster was the smirk of Brant. It culminated in a last-ditch effort to be a hero and yeah, that went south and worse, McDonald got shot. The Met were in dire straits and desperately needed good press so they managed to have McDonald appear some sort of half-arsed hero, and though he kept his job, he was a figure of derision to the others. A leper in blue, to be avoided, and the Super, just buying time till he quietly dumped him.

Meantime, he was drawing all the shite assignments and like, who was he gonna call? The duties usually given to rookies were now thrown to him. His current brief? Standing outside shopping centres, giving directions to pissed-off pedestrians. He needed something major, something biblical, to turn his career around, but for the life of him, he couldn't come up with anything. Nigh resigned to his fate, he'd begun looking at security guard advertisements, truly, the bottom rung of a cop's descent into hell.

WPC Andrews was the exact opposite of McDonald. She was relatively new, had gotten the break he'd dreamed about, she'd been a reluctant hero, and even Falls, who cut slack for nobody, seemed to almost like her. On hearing about Brant, she began to weep, she still bought the crap, how the downing of one of their own diminished them all. She actually voiced this to Chief Inspector Roberts, who looked at her like she was mad. She put this down to shock, she knew how close he was to Brant.

Close!

That would be stretching it. They had history, lots of it, primarily bad, but they were connected, Brant continually

managed to amaze Roberts, the risks he took, his whole attitude to the world fascinated and appalled Roberts. The chief
inspector stared at Andrews, her fresh face, the whole gung ho
spirit, he wanted to tell her he wasn't surprised Brant had
been shot, **simply dismayed it had taken so long.** You
danced on the edge like Brant did, they were going to get
you, and that was just the good guys.

He asked:

'I'm on my way over to the hospital. You want a lift?'

She was delighted. They could share and bond, form a special relationship born of grief and empathy, and he wasn't un-
attractive, plus, it would add to her cred, heighten her profile.

They were on their way out when Foley, the desk sergeant, called Roberts, who snapped:

'Not now, for heaven's sake, Brant has been shot.'

Foley wanted to protest:

'Hey, don't bite my bloody head off. You think I don't
hurt, don't I bleed too, am I not human?'

He'd recently seen *The Elephant Man* and had been pro-
foundly affected. There was other whiny stuff he wanted to
say but felt it wouldn't fly, he'd keep it for his wife and, who
knew, he might even get another of them pity shags. Instead,
he adopted his officious tone, let the bastard know he knew
what was important, said:

'I wouldn't, of course, have bothered you, sir, at such a
moment . . .'

Paused.

Ammunition

Let the hard leak all over the words, then:

'But the caller said he had information on the shooting.'

Roberts looked like he might hit him, and the sergeant backed off a little. Roberts barked:

'There isn't anyone else in the whole station to take the call? Every nutter in South-East London is going to be on the blower claiming he did it. Surely you're capable of taking a message your own self, you've been sat on yer arse long enough to know.'

The slur of being a desk jockey was not lost, and the sergeant let that hang for a moment then said, in an icy voice:

'Yes sir, and I wouldn't have bothered you in your moment of tremendous urgency, but the caller did specify you by name and my years of sitting on my . . . rear . . . tell me he's genuine.'

He was well pleased with this, felt it said:

'Fuck you, Jack, and proper.'

Roberts sighed, brushed past the sergeant, grabbed the phone, spat:

'This is Roberts.'

Heard:

'So terribly loath to bother you at a time of obviously deep distress and trauma.'

The voice was rich, cultured, what used to be called a BBC accent, not to mention extremely posh. It immediately got up Roberts's nose. He demanded:

'You have information on a shooting?'

His impatience, testiness, was palpable and answered by a full chuckle, it wasn't laughter, no, it was the sound of someone who was delighted at the response. He mimicked Roberts:

'"*A shooting.*" You jest, my good fellow. Surely it's *the shooting,* or am I overrating the value of our esteemed Detective Sergeant Brant?'

Roberts was gripping the receiver so hard it hurt the palm of his hand. He tried to loosen up in every sense, asked:

'You have information, is that right?'

Again, the chuckle, a real fun guy, then:

'Well, old bean, it's not a social call, pleasurable as that would no doubt be, this is indeed a call with information. Might there be a financial incentive for me to, as they say, "spill the beans."'

Roberts was signalling for the desk sergeant to get a trace on the call. The sergeant ignored him, elected not to know what Roberts meant with his furious hand gestures. See how he liked to be fucked with.

Roberts said into the phone:

'Any citizen helping the police will be entitled to the full gratitude of the Met?'

Even Roberts knew this sounded like a crock, and the guy said:

'Tut tut, Chief Inspector, the party line, what? I'll expect a more enlightened approach when next I call.'

Roberts nigh panicked, rushed:

'What's the information? How do I know you're not just some nut case?'

Silence and Roberts thought the guy was gone, then:

'You'll discover the weapon was a Browning Automatic, the full clip was . . . employed . . . and my deepest apologies for the somewhat . . . how shall we say, scatter-gun theatrics, but good help is so hard to find, I'm sure you have similar difficulties with staff. If a next time is required, I shall try to ensure a little more finesse.'

Roberts realised he was sweating, tried:

' "Next time." What the hell does that mean?'

There was a burst of static on the line, then the guy said:

'If perchance our beloved Sergeant Brant hasn't cashed in his chips, then we shall have to try again, persistence being the quality we can all aspire to. For now, tootle-pip.'

Roberts wanted to scream, *'tootle-pip'*? Who the fuck talked like that outside of the pages of a P. G. Wodehouse novel. He gasped:

'But why, why Sergeant Brant?'

A full baritone laugh, then:

'Your attempts to keep me on the line are admirable if a tad amateurish, but as to why, really, Chief Inspector, can you honestly think of anyone who doesn't want to shoot the said misfortunate?'

Click.

The bastard was gone.

Roberts whirled round to the desk jockey, shouted:

'Did you trace him?'

The sergeant asked:

'Oh, did you want a trace?'

Roberts nearly went over the desk, reined it in a bit, said:

'That's what my bloody hand signals were for, you moron.'

The sergeant, not missing a beat, said:

'Ah, I thought you were asking for tea? Speaking of which, shall I order you up a nice cuppa, you seem a touch overwrought?'

Roberts spun on his heel, snapped at Andrews:

'What are you standing around for, bring the damn car.'

Andrews felt it was a bit ripe to take it out on her, but kept her thoughts to herself.

Roberts comforted himself with the thought that all calls into the station were recorded as a matter of course and maybe they'd get something off those. He ordered the desk guy to have the tapes in his office . . . pronto.

The desk sergeant muttered:

'*Seig Heil.*'

3

FALLS WAS BETWEEN exhilaration and depression. One moment she wanted to scream in triumph, then was plunged into the depths. Her third attempt, she'd passed the sergeants' exam.

Well, cheated on the sergeants' exam.

Brant had gotten the papers for her, and she'd made the requisite protest when he'd offered to get them. She'd said:

'Oh, I can't do that.'

Brant had given his wolf smile, said:

'Fine, but you'll fail again and guess what, babe, there ain't going to be a fourth try.'

That she had to agree was true on both counts, she said:

'I've been studying, really trying.'

Brant laughed out loud, said:

'Bollocks. You're black, they already have their quota of minorities in place and you, you've got some very . . . *colourful* . . . form.'

No argument there, she'd more screwups than Liza Minnelli, so she had to ask:

'And what will it cost me?'

You did business with Brant, it always cost, a lot, and if it was only money but no, something you had to compromise yourself with. He said:

'I'll think of something.'

She asked:

'How will you get the papers?'

He laughed out loud, then:

'Do you really want to know?'

She didn't, and he said:

'Thought so.'

Then he added:

'Sergeant.'

And here it was, the official confirmation of it. All those years of slogging away and now she was Sergeant Falls. Years ago, she'd been the wet dream of the nick, all the coppers had the hots for her, and her blackness only added to her appeal. But the job, the job had turned her into a female Brant almost, and the appreciation of her went down the toilet. And the new bitch, Andrews, she was the current prize. Falls had fallen prey to coke, booze, and she knew they suspected she'd had some involvement in the death of a notorious cop killer. She'd managed to block that whole episode out of her head.

Sometimes, in her nightmares, she'd see a hammer and on waking, drenched in sweat, she'd resolve not to dwell on it, muttering:

'Just more bad shit.'

The past was not so much another country as a minefield of horror. She shook herself, physically ridding her psyche of bad karma, whispered:

'Moving on, girl.'

Focused on her new status . . . Sergeant . . . Sergeant Falls, had a ring to it, the ring of a winner. The phone went and she figured Brant. The price to pay. It was Porter Nash. They'd been the best of mates once, minorities battling together.

Hadn't lasted.

Mores the Brixton-ed pity.

Porter Nash got right to it, said:

'Brant's been shot.'

Hit her like a . . . hammer?

Took her a moment to grasp, and she asked:

'Is he . . . ?'

Porter said:

'He's in intensive care. We won't know for a few hours yet.'

He gave her the name of the hospital, and she said she'd be right over. It was after she'd put the phone down that she realized she'd forgotten to tell Porter she'd made the grade. Didn't look like there'd be any party to celebrate now and, hating herself, she thought maybe she wouldn't have to repay Brant, then said aloud:

'Get a grip, Sergeant.'

How to dress for a hospital? She went with her off-duty gear: jeans, plain sweatshirt, sneakers, but hold a mo. Hospital, cute doctors, right? She went with short skirt, medium heels,

some light lippy, and her best jacket, a black blazer, it accentu-
ated her colour, and gave her that casual style that seemed like
an afterthought, not the hours of agony it had been. A doctor
seeing her was going to go:

'Hold the bloody transfusions.'

Yeah, that was going to happen.

Checking the mirror with total concentration, she found
new lines around her eyes and lied:

'Laughter ones, is all.'

Her life had been such *fun*. It was only surprising she
hadn't more, lines that is. Her car, a newish Datsun, had an
envelope stuck under the wiper, she reckoned, pizza flyer or
such till she saw the handwriting on the front, it read

GIRLFRIEND.

With a sinking heart, she got in the car, looked nervously
round, then got the hell out of there.

4

WALKING INTO THE hospital, Falls clocked the number of cops, uniforms everywhere, flasks of coffee.

And hookers.

A whole gaggle of them

Falls had never seen so many in one place since her last patrol along Kings Cross and, even more noteworthy, they were quiet.

Silence and hookers are not usually in the same neighbourhood. Falls knew the older ones and approached them, asked:

'What's happening, girls?'

The younger ones sneered at her, but Beth, a veteran, said:

'We're here for Brant.'

Wait till the press got hold of that. Falls knew Brant would be delighted, asked:

'Any news?'

Beth glanced at the group of officers in a corner, said:

'Sure, those pricks are keeping us right up to date.'

Falls nearly smiled, and Beth added:

'Most of them are shit scared I'll call them by their first names and I might yet.'

Falls said she'd see what she could learn, and Beth looked at her, said:

'Lose the blazer.'

Porter detached himself from the brass, came to Falls, snapped:

'What kept you?'

Falls knew of the odd friendship between him and Brant, but he didn't need to take it out on her. She lashed back:

'You called me twenty minutes ago. What you'd think, I'd fucking fly over?'

He backed off, said:

'There's no news yet, he's still in intensive care, I have to go to the station, be debriefed, I was with Brant when he got hit.'

Falls went into cop mode, asked:

'Did you see the shooter?'

Porter, his face drawn, said:

'It happened so quickly, I never got a chance.'

Falls considered that, then said as she moved away:

'Too busy saving your own skin.'

Roberts arrived, with Andrews in tow, looked stunned to see the hooker convention, and moved to the officers, said:

'Get them out of here.'

One of the younger guys said:

'They might make a scene.'

Roberts gave him his full gaze, said:

'Don't give me fucking lip, give me results.'

He grabbed Porter, heard how the shooting went down, then:

'I had a call from the shooter.'

Porter was astonished, asked:

'Did he say why?'

Roberts couldn't believe the stupidity, said:

' 'Cos it's fucking Brant, why'd you think?'

Roberts asked if Brant had any family, and Porter said:

'We thought you'd be the most likely to know, you being his mate and all.'

Roberts blew that off, said:

'Nobody is Brant's mate. Haven't you learnt anything?'

Roberts did know there'd been a wife and eventually got one of the officers to track her down, got the phone number, and Porter volunteered:

'If you wish, sir, I can make the call.'

Trying to regain some ground, he felt Roberts had never liked him.

He was right.

Roberts, the mobile in his hand, stopped, asked:

'Do you know her?'

'No, sir.'

'Then why the fuck would *you* call her?'

And turned away. He dialled the number and a woman answered. He explained who he was and in what he hoped was a sympathetic tone, explained what had happened, she cut him off with:

'Is he dead?'

'No, thank god . . .'

'Call me when he is.'

Click.

Stunned, Roberts stared at the phone. Porter was hovering, asked:

'How did she take it?'

'Real well. She sounded like she won the lottery.'

They say all coppers are bastards. They're not—but those that are make a very good job of it.
                                        —Charlie Kray

5

TERRY DUNNE WAS nervous. Not a good feeling for a hit man to have. He'd been in the business for over two years, making a nice rep, building it slow and steady. He'd done a few criminals, guys who'd crossed the wrong people, got greedy, and got whacked. No civilians and, so far, no heat. The cops treated it as almost a service when someone took the wrong uns off the board. So he'd stayed under the radar, his name known to the men who mattered.

When he'd got the assignment for Brant, he'd nearly said no. A cop is a whole other league and the fallout was ferocious, but if you want to move up? Too, the guy who took Brant out was going to be legend, could double, shit, triple his fees. There wasn't a major villain in South-East London who didn't want Brant out of the picture. But the bastard, maybe it was his Irish blood, he had the luck of the very devil. Terry had gone along to meet with the man who wanted the hit, he'd been picked up by a BMW on the Clapham Road, and just one occupant in the car, the driver.

He'd opened the door, asked:

Ammunition

'Terry Dunne?'

When Terry Dunne nodded, the guy said:

'Hop in, old chap.'

Spoke like a Tory outrider, and he had the looks to match. In his forties, with a ruddy face, prominent nose, beady eyes, and an air of . . . what did they call it in the posh papers . . . yeah, *bonhomie*. Terry learned that word in Scrabble with his old lady. She was a bitch for them frog words, but he'd liked the ring of it, used it every chance. Mind you, the pubs, clubs of Brixton, Kennington, Stockwell, you didn't get to use it much. Unless you wanted your card marked as pillow biter. You used a word like that, you better be carrying.

The man drove them to Canary Wharf, asking:

'You're not in a hurry old bean, are you?'

Not if he was being paid and, as if reading his thoughts, the guy said:

'You will, of course, be amply rewarded for your time.'

Terry got a good look at him, sneakily, of course, didn't pay to be too inquisitive. He wondered if the guy was a messenger but doubted it, he had the air of being the main contractor, Terry was surprised, usually, all sorts of middle men were involved. The guy brought the car to a smooth stop on the wharf, asked:

'Are you at all cognisant with Detective Sergeant Brant?'

Cognisant?

Fuck.

He said:

'Who isn't?'

The man gave a loud laugh, far too loud and forced for what was essentially a simple truthful reply. He said:

'Touché, well said, my learned friend. It means we won't have to bandy words with explanations, motivations, not that you much care for motive, am I correct in my wild assumption?'

Terry had to concentrate to follow what the bastard was actually saying. He settled for 'Yeah.'

Truth was, the guy was kind of creepy. You knew if you touched him—and who'd want to?—he'd be ice cold. The guy took out a slim gold cigarette case, extracted a long cigarillo, offered the case, and Terry shook his head. The guy asked:

'Mind if I indulge?'

Like it would matter

Terry said, letting a slight hint of impatience in there:

'Your dime, mate.'

The man mimicked.

' "Mate." I like it, gives that working-class zing of authenticity, methinks you have sly humour there, *mon ami*.'

He lit the cig with a gold Zippo, the clink of the lighter sounding loud and final. He blew out a cloud of smoke, said:

'Well, to business, you're a busy man I'm sure, I'll pay you ten large to . . . remove the aforementioned chap. Two now and the rest on completion.'

Terry felt it was time to take control, said:

'Oh oh, I get half up front.'

The guy turned in his seat, let Terry see his eyes, washed out blue, as if they'd been bleached. He said in a tone of pure ice:

'I don't negotiate with the help. You usually get five for the whole performance, I'm doubling your fee.'

Terry was intimidated but then moved in his seat, the Browning in his belt giving him balls, said:

'He's a cop, a very high-profile one.'

The guy lowered his window, tossed the cig, said:

'Get out.'

Terry had to decide fast, went with:

'Three now.'

The guy was staring straight ahead, repeated:

'I don't negotiate.'

Terry thought, fuck it, and said:

'Okay.'

Then Terry fucked it up, emptied a whole clip at Brant and the word was, the bastard was still alive, in Intensive Care sure but . . . not dead. And now Terry had to meet with the posh geezer. Didn't figure he'd be getting the rest of his money. He'd reloaded the Browning, jammed it in his jacket, and went to the Clapham Road to wait.

The BMW was right on time and he got in, his excuses ready and his pledge to finish the job and . . . and fuck.

To his amazement, the guy was breezy, asked:

'And how are we today?'

He sounded downright cheerful, maybe he'd heard Brant

croaked? You never knew in this biz, luck, rarely, evident but just possible. He let his tension ease a notch, said:

'Bit of a cock-up, alas.'

The guy laughed, actually tapped Terry's knee, said:

'Hey, no problem, my man. Could happen to the best of us.'

Terry wondered if the guy was a fruit, a lot of these Public School guys, buggery was part of the curriculum. They were heading for Canary Wharf again. The guy eased the car into a space, looked round, said:

'No prying eyes, one must practise due diligence.'

Terry told him of how the unexpected had happened and the customer had knocked his aim off. The guy listening, his face conveying understanding. Then he asked:

'You have the weapon with you?'

Terry wasn't sure where this was going, said:

'Am, yeah.'

'May I see it?'

Terry took the weapon out and the guy put out his hand, saying:

'I trust it's primed, reloaded?'

Reluctantly, Terry let go of the gun, said:

'Of course.'

The guy examined it, said:

'Seems to be fine, must be you.'

Took Terry a moment, then he said:

'I'll put it right, don't you worry about that.'

The guy gave him a full look, asked:

'Do I look worried to you?' Then he shot Terry three times in the stomach, said:

'See, nothing wrong with it.'

Terry saw the blood seep out of his belly, ruining his good jeans, and he knew they'd be a bitch to clean, the guy said:

'Gut shot, they say it's agony, are they right?'

They were.

Then the guy leaned over, shoved Terry on the ground, and got out himself, he said:

'Call this early retirement and here's your bonus.'

Put two more in Terry's skull. Stared at the body, said:

'Golly gosh, that is messy.'

He got back in the car, eased into first gear, backed up, then drove carefully away. He was humming the theme from the *Bridge over the River Kwai,* always a favourite of his.

6

McDONALD WAS FREEZING his nuts off. The cold
weather had come with a goddamn vengeance and no matter
where he stood, the cold seemed to seek him out, lash him.
He was outside the Shopping Centre in Balham, wondering
if he'd risk hopping off for a coffee when a group of hoodies
passed, teenagers with the hoods pulled up to cover their
faces. You couldn't tell if they were male or female. As they
moved by, one of them spat on his shoes.

He lost it, grabbed the figure, dashed him against the wall,
said:

'You want to play games, how'd you like this one, called
headbanging.'

He let go and the hood had slipped, revealing a girl, in her
late teens, her forehead pouring blood, one of the boys
whined:

'Why'd you do that?'

McDonald smiled, said:

'Because I can, now get the hell out of here.'

They slumped off, muttering darkly. A pensioner had been

watching and McDonald figured, here we go, the old geezer
will report me. Did he care? Not a lot. The man said:

'Let me shake your hand.'

And did.

McDonald was astonished, said:

'Thank you.'

The man beamed, said:

'That's the spirit that put the Great in Britain.'

McDonald asked:

'Fancy a cup of tea, a bacon sarnie?'

Roberts and Porter were still at the hospital, a doctor approached, asked:

'Who's the ranking officer?'

He was looking at Porter, as if he knew it was him, so
Porter, said:

'That would be Chief Inspector Roberts here.'

The doctor was disappointed, sighed, said to Roberts:

'We've got the bullet out and he will be okay, but we're
keeping him in Intensive Care for twenty-four hours, purely
precautionary.'

Roberts let his chest relax, didn't realise how tight he'd
been holding himself, Porter said:

'Thank Christ.'

The doctor asked:

'Has his family been informed?'

Before Porter could speak, Roberts said:

'We're his family.'

The doctor thought, poor bastard, and Roberts asked him:

'What about headaches?'

The doctor was puzzled, said:

'He was shot in the back, I don't think it will necessarily cause headaches.'

Roberts stared at him, said:

'Not Brant. Me, my head is opening.'

The doctor paused, then:

'You'll find a pharmacy on the ground floor.'

And stomped off

Roberts said:

'Pompous bugger.'

Porter said:

'The superintendent hasn't shown.'

Roberts said:

'He doesn't know.'

Porter couldn't believe it, said:

'I don't believe it. Shouldn't he be informed?'

Roberts was rubbing the front of his face, looking tired, said:

'You're so worried, you call him.'

Took a while to locate the superintendent, but eventually Porter was given his mobile number by a very irate secretary who cautioned:

'You better have a very valid reason for disturbing him.'

And hung up.

The Super answered with a gruff:

'Who the hell is this?'

Not a very promising opening, Porter ploughed on:

'It's Porter Nash, sir.'

Silence for a moment, then:

'I'm in the middle of a round of golf. This better be good.'

Porter took a deep breath, said:

'Sergeant Brant has been shot.'

No hesitation now:

'Is he dead?'

'No, sir, he's going to pull through, thank god.'

Porter could hear Brown tell someone else and presumed he was already pulling out all the stops, getting all personnel mobilized, Brown said:

'You might thank god, laddie, others would see it differently.'

Porter knew that Brant had been a constant problem to Brown and all the brass, but he'd expected at least a show of vague concern.

Nope.

Wasn't going to get it. He tried to keep the anger out of his voice, asked:

'Would you like the details of the shooting, sir?'

'You think they'll improve my chances of getting on the green in less than two strokes?'

Roberts was staring at Porter, obviously aware of how it was going, Porter said:

'No sir, I don't see how it could possibly improve your . . . performance.'

Porter could have been mistaken but he heard what sounded awfully like a titter?

Brown said:

'Tell Roberts, he's his mate, if an animal like Brant could be said to have such. Personally I doubt it.'

Click.

Roberts watched Porter slam the mobile on the palm of his hand, said:

'He was full of concern I'd guess.'

Porter wanted to hit somebody, said:

'He was full of shit is what he was.'

Roberts thought there might be hope for Porter yet and asked him if he fancied a pint? And to his astonishment, Porter agreed, giving his number to the nurses station lest there be any change. On their way out, a large man stopped them, asked in a Yank accent:

'How's our boy doing?'

Porter said:

'He's going to be fine, you want to come for a jar?'

'Is that like a beer?'

Roberts, already out of all patience, snapped:

'Do we look like we're going for a cup of tea?'

And kept moving. The Yank looked to Porter who just shook his head and indicated he should just trail along.

He did.

Ammunition

They went to the Black Lion, recently taken over by a re-tired cop named Sully. They got a table at the rear and Sully limped over, the cause of his retirement. He said:

'Real sorry to hear about Brant.'

Roberts said:

'Yeah, bring me a large Scotch and whatever these fellahs want?'

The Yank went into a long query about the variety of beers, and Roberts said:

'Hey, can you get to it, we've had a long fucking day. You want to drink or write a fucking column on ale?'

The Yank was delighted, hostility was his favourite gig. He said:

'Bring me a pint of that bitter you guys drink, and any chance it might be like chilled.'

Sully said:

'Not a chance in hell.'

Porter ordered a gin and slim-line tonic, the other two giving him a withering look.

There was a silence as they waited for the drinks, Roberts tapped his fingers on the table, irritating them all, himself most of all, but no one commented.

Porter said:

'I'd kill for a fag.'

He had been diagnosed as diabetic so cigs were out, but it didn't stop the craving, in fact, not being able to made it worse. Roberts laughed and Porter realized what he'd said . . .

36

thought, uh-oh, *Fag for a fag*. It eased the tension, and the Yank put out his hand to Roberts, said:

'We haven't been introduced, I'm L. M. Wallace and you're Roberts, the chief inspector?'

Roberts reluctantly took his hand, said:

'I know who you are, you're going to tell us how to run things, just what we need.'

The drinks came, Roberts was reaching for his wallet but Wallace beat him to it, said:

'My treat.'

He raised the pint, inspected it, then said:

'I'm not here to tell you jack shit, buddy. I'm here in an advisory position, not my idea I can tell you that, I could be back home, watching the Yankees having their ass handed to them.'

Porter raised his glass, said:

'Hey, here's to cooperation, right?'

Roberts drained his shot in one, shouted:

'Sully, same again.'

Wallace clinked his glass against Porter's, said:

'Here's looking at you, bro.'

He knocked off most of the pint in one toss, said:

'Jesus H. Christ, that's piss.'

Then he settled back in his chair, asked:

'So, who shot your sergeant?'

Are we all bare-faced liars?
—Jonathan Aiken,
gaoled Tory minister

7

FALLS HAD FINALLY left the hospital, the nurse telling her Brant was comfortable and got the look from Falls, who asked:

'He was shot in the back a few hours ago and he's comfortable?'

The nurse, white, was never entirely at ease with black people, they seemed so angry all the time. She ventured:

'It's what we say, you know, to reassure the relatives.'

Falls was beginning to enjoy the mind fuck, asked:

'You noticed that Sergeant Brant is white?'

'Am . . . yes.'

Falls took her time, then:

'So, how do you figure I'm related to him?'

The nurse fled.

Falls headed for the pub, she had her new rank to celebrate, went to The Oval pub right beside the station, bought a copy of The Big Issue from the homeless guy, who said:

'Sorry to hear about Brant.'

'Course, word would have spread all over the South-East,

Brant downed at last. She muttered something, and the guy interpreted it as *keep the change*. She liked this pub, no cops, lots of villains, but then where didn't?

The barman, surly git, growled:

'What will it be?'

He hadn't twigged her for the heat, or he'd have changed his tone. Falls said:

'Large gin and tonic and a pack of B & H.'

The guy sniggered, said:

'See that machine over there, the one that says "cigarettes" in large bright letters, guess what it's for?'

Falls was tired, and the letter in her bag was burning a hole. She leaned over to the guy, said:

'I'm Sergeant Falls, and I'm in a real fucking bad frame of mind, so how about you bring me what I ordered. I'll be sitting over there in the corner.'

He did.

Even had the cellophone off the packet, one of the cigs perked up, Falls gave him a tenner and poured a tiny hint of the tonic in the glass, no need to screw up perfectly fine gin with tonic. She knocked back a sizeable wallop, sat back, waited for the jolt. It came fast and she let out a barely audible sigh. The guy brought her change and she snapped:

'Same again.'

She was going to be massacred, see what the night would produce then. She waited till she was half through her second double before she allowed herself to think about the letter.

A time back, the Vixen case, a particularly nasty psycho named Angie, who took out two brothers and countless more they only suspected. Worse, she had deliberately targeted Falls, became her friend. And Falls, she cringed, despite the gin, blushed, . . . Jesus, the memory . . . on one very drunken occasion . . . her lover. It had nigh on destroyed her career and only a miracle in the form of Brant had saved her arse.

Angie was caught and pulled down heavy jail time. Falls had breathed a sigh of relief and only hoped some other crazy bitch would put a shiv in Angie's back. She opened the latter, realized her hands were shaking, read:

Girlfriend,
How are you sweetie?
I've missed you.
Your black, creamy skin, your wild, abandoned love-making, your lovely face got me through so rough times here on her
Majesty's Service.
Wonderful news.
I'm out.
Aren't you delighted?
I know you are.
I know you long for me.
Patience, my black meat.
I have few a loose ends to put right, but then I'll be round. I see you're still at the same address.
We'll make up for all the lost time.

Ammunition

Soon, my lover.
Be patient.

Xxxxxxxx

Your own fox

Falls wiped her brow, sweat was pouring off her, the gin she hoped. The bar guy was over, asked:

'Hot enough for yah?'

Falls fixed her steel eyes on him, said:

'Fuck off.'

He loved it, said:

'God, I love it when babes talk dirty.'

And he was gone before Falls could reply.

She couldn't believe it, Angie was out and stalking her. Panic gripped her. Angie was among the craziest of a whole series of deranged lunatics she'd met in her time on the force.

And to say she had *ammunition* on Falls was putting it mildly. Falls lit a cigarette, her hands a little steadier. The only person who could really deal with this type of psycho was Brant.

Feeling the drinks, Falls got to her feet and wondered if she should call a cab, she wasn't sure if she was in any shape to drive.

The bar guy said:

'You come back and cheer us all up soon, you hear.'

Brant would have given him a wallop up the side of the head.

8

McDONALD WAS HOME, shaking his head in disbelief. The events of the day had staggered him. Just when he truly believed his life was fully in the toilet, the cavalry had arrived—in the guise of an old codger.

Go figure.

After he had bashed the young hooded girl and invited the old man for a cuppa, it had never once occurred to him that his whole future was about to change. They'd gone to a transport caff, one of the few real English places still existing, the old man prattling on about the country having gone to the dogs . . . though he might have well said . . . *wogs.*

Which meant he had either a lisp or a serious hard-on for foreigners. They'd ordered bacon sarnies, a neon-lit nightmare of carbos, and, of course, a large pot of tea, brewed with Lipton's real tea, none of that tea-bag shite. The sandwiches arrived, dripping fat and lard, just the way McDonald adored them. As they ate, with relish, the old man, mid bite, asked:

Ammunition

'So, how come a bright young copper like yourself is pulling garbage duty?'

McDonald thought about giving him a sob story but decided to tell the truth, said:

'There's no tolerance any more for hands-on policing.'

This seemed to be exactly the answer the old man was hoping for. He extended his hand, said:

'I'm Bill Traynor, fought for my country and what do I get?'

McDonald put three sugars in his tea, ventured:

'Sweet fanny all I'd say.'

Bill was nodding, said:

'Too bloody right, mate. Where I live, we're tormented by young Pakis, playing loud music, insulting our wives, sneering at us as we go to the post office, and don't even mention the darkies. They wait for us to collect our pensions, not that you could feed a frigging cat on what they give us, and they jump us after we collect.'

He was gasping for breath, took out an inhaler, said:

'Me bloody lungs are shot but before I go, I'd like to make a stand, are you following me?'

McDonald had a fair idea but he'd let Bill spit it out, said nothing and simply stirred his tea:

Bill looked round, then said, in nearly a whisper:

'A group of us have formed an association, a band of men to take back our streets, but we're old, how effective can we be.'

He stared at McDonald, and seeing nothing to warrant handcuffs, took the plunge, said:

'Now if we had a bright young ballsy fellah to lead us, we might make a difference, do you follow me so far?'

McDonald thought how complicated was it, a bunch of pensioner vigilantes, he nearly laughed but Bill added:

'We'd pay the right man to lead us, pay him well.'

McDonald, his face neutral, asked:

'Define *well*?'

Bill mentioned a figure that took McDonald by surprise. The truth was, he'd have done it gratis just to have some respect, even if it was old respect.

Bill was fidgeting, nervous as a rat, asked:

'What do you think?'

McDonald smiled, asked:

'When would you like to begin?'

They'd decided on Friday night, that was the worst time, when the nonnationals got weeded up, doped up, boozed up, and went amok. McDonald had written down a shopping list for Bill, said:

'This is what we'll need for openers.'

Bill scanned the list, his dentures spreading in a wide smile.

Baseball bats
Balaclavas
Petrol
Billiard balls

Ammunition

Bill had hesitated at the last item, asked:

'What's the balls for?'

McDonald drained the last of his tea, timing being vital, said, as he stood up:

'We're going to make the bastards eat them.'

Bill loved it.

McDonald had picked up a fairly serious coke habit after he'd been shot and was fond of the jolt of speed too. He did a line now, swallowed a tab of speed, and as the drugs wired him, he said aloud:

'The boy is back in town.'

Put his favourite Thin Lizzy album on the sound system, cranked it to max, punched the air in a little victory jig.

The people who lived below would have complained, but who were they going to call? The cops?

Roberts, Porter Nash, and Wallace were still in the pub. Roberts had put away twice the amount of booze as the others, then stood up, threw a slew of notes on the table, said:

'I better hit the road, we've a lot of suspects to track down tomorrow.'

Porter noticed Roberts was unsteady on his feet and tried:

'You okay to get home?'

Roberts glared at him, asked:

'And what, you going to walk me?'

Porter recognized the sheer belligerence of the aggressive drunk, ready to lash out at anyone. He reined in, said:

'No, just if you wanted a cab or something?'

Roberts eyed him, then said:

'You want something to fret about, then worry about finding who shot Brant, there's a good boy.'

And he was gone.

There was silence till Wallace asked:

'Apart from his sergeant being shot, what's the other bug up his ass?'

Seeing Porter smile, he realized what he'd said, went:

'Sorry, buddy, I didn't mean anything personal.'

Porter was used to the double entendres and let them slide, said:

'The chief inspector lost his wife a time ago, then he hit a series of real success in his cases until he went after a villain alone.'

Wallace just loved the way the Brits talked . . . *villains* . . . back home they called them perps, skels but this, this was almost cosy. He asked:

'You up for a nightcap, one for the road?'

Porter had already had way more than he should, with diabetes, he shouldn't even be drinking but thought, what the hell, said:

'Yeah, let's go for it.'

Wallace went to the bar, came back with two shot glasses,

full to the brim. Porter watched him carry the glasses in his huge fists, never spilling a drop, and saw the hard muscle beneath the bulk, and knew, despite Wallace's affability, this was one hard case. Wallace put the shots on the table, said:

'Buddy, I couldn't believe it, they had Jim Beam. Down in one, you game?'

He was and they tossed them back, Porter waited a moment and then gave a shudder, the bourbon hit his stomach like a train, an express. His eyes watered, Wallace laughed, said:

'Gets you where you live, am I right?'

Porter didn't know was it the alcohol or exhaustion but he liked this guy, liked him a lot, asked:

'So what exactly are you supposed to be doing here, besides getting the locals bombed on bourbon.'

He wished he hadn't used the term *bombed* with an antiterrorist expert but it was late. If Wallace had caught it, he let it slide, said:

'Well, I'm supposed to get you guys up to speed on how to spot suspects, how to respond, and Jesus H. Christ, god forbid, we get a situation, what the emergency measures are.'

Porter considered this, then asked:

'Off the top of your head, what's the best advice you can give?'

Wallace didn't hesitate, said:

'Shoot the motherfuckers.'

Outside the pub, Wallace said:

'Man, I could eat me a leg of steer, anyplace open?'

Porter suggested the fish and chipper, the Chinese, and then said:

' 'Course, the new tradition, after you sink a fair few, is to get a kebab and come tomorrow, you'll wish you were dead.'

Wallace was delighted, offered to treat Porter to one, but Porter cried off, said:

'I better get home. Thanks for the company, I enjoyed it.'

Wallace gave him an odd look, then:

'I think you mean it, buddy. You're okay, fellah. I heard you were a pillow biter, and I don't have any beef with that, but I wasn't planning on hooking up with you, so yeah, it was good. You take real good care now, we got us some bad hombres to catch.'

As Porter walked home, the booze giving him a lift, he tried to remember if Wallace was from Texas or New York. He was certainly from another planet.

This is how we get in trouble, we talk.

—John Gotti

9

FOR THE NEXT week, the cops did what they do best . . . knocked on doors, the old reliable, and checked out various tips that were phoned in. Brant had been moved out of Intensive Care and was now in a private room with two armed policemen outside. The doctors were stunned at his rate of recovery. He was on his feet by the second day but eerily silent. The Super had sent a flunkey to wish him a speedy recovery, Brant told him to get fucked. The flunkey didn't report these exact words. He knew that in the Met, they did shoot the messenger, he simply said that Brant was healing rapidly.

The Super sighed.

Roberts, with WPC Andrews along, went to find Brant's current snitch, a colourful individual named Caz, who wore garish shirts and, oddly enough, had never done any jail time. He was known to be a consummate dancer, though how this enriched his profession of snitching was up for debate. He carried a switchblade and was reputed to be very fast with said instrument.

Caz had met Roberts before, but was not happy to see yet another cop, especially a woman. They found him in The Warrington Arms, drinking a shandy. He looked at Roberts, ignoring Andrews, whined:

'Who da bitch?'

He was from Croydon but affected to be from Salvador, Equador, Argentina, depending on the day of the week. Roberts sat in right beside Caz, Andrews opposite, and he stomped down hard on Caz's right foot, saying:

'She's a police person. Don't call her that again . . . *claro, amigo*?'

Caz yelped, that was his best foot for the rumba. He said:

'How I can operate as undercover for you, you keep exposing me to new coppers?'

The barman was heading their way but Roberts waved him off, said to Caz:

'Drop the accent and the attitude. You fuck with that lady, you fuck with me, got it?'

Caz got it.

Andrews had never met a snitch before, and Roberts had told her that they were the poisoned life blood of policing, but you had to treat them with a delicate balance of intimidation and flattery. She had no idea of how this could work.

Mostly, it was the intimidation.

Roberts had added, when they least expect it, you bung them a few quid. Andrews was horrified, asked:

'The Met pays them?'

Roberts let out a breath, said:

'No, we pay them out of petty cash, off the books.'

Andrews was still of the belief that policing was a higher calling and that a certain code of morals should be followed. She said:

'But isn't that wrong?'

Roberts looked at her, wondering how long before she grew up, said:

'It's wrong if we don't get the information.'

She watched Caz. He seemed like a totally unreliable sort. She wouldn't believe a word he said and . . . him calling her a bitch, there was no cause for that. Roberts was asking:

'So, my dancing ponce, who shot our sergeant?'

Saw Caz's eyes shift and knew, bingo, the bastard knew. Roberts was astonished, he knew Caz had access to information that others could only dream of but this fast? He kept his face in neutral as Caz extended his sympathy, saying how much he respected the sergeant and Roberts let him ramble on for a few minutes, then snarled:

'I asked you a question?'

Caz looked at Andrews, a lecherous smile building, asked:

'There is a reward, no, I mean, a shot policeman, this is major event.'

Roberts had to bite down on his desire to reach over and throttle the snitch. He said:

'Oh yeah. You help bring in a cop shooter, you're talking major recompense.'

Ammunition

Caz had been promised rewards before and usually ended up with a sore jaw after Brant had dished out his form of compensation. Caz sat back, said:

'I thought so, so how about we have a little good faith cash up front?'

Roberts sighed, Jesus, he was tired, tired of having to deal with scum, said:

'You give me the name, you'll be paid. You know how it works.'

Caz weighed his options then on impulse, gave it up, said:

'Terry Dunne, he's the one did the shooting.'

Andrews was amazed, could it be so easy, you went to a snitch and he solved your case.

Roberts asked:

'And this piece of work, where do we find him?'

Caz laughed, not a pretty sound, more like a cackle, asked:

'Am I to do all your work, Chief Inspector? He's local, but that's all I know.'

Roberts mobile shrilled and he stood up, said:

'I'll take this outside.'

Andrews wasn't wild about being left alone with the low-life and was even more bothered when Caz gave her his full-wattage smile, a blend of malice and lust, he asked:

'You like dancing, chiquita?'

She wasn't going to get into a conversation with this creep, snapped:

'No.'

He loved it, leaned over, his hand poised to touch hers, said:

'You have not been with the maestro, I meet you Saturday night, I take you the Crystal, show you some steps, and after, ah . . . after, *mi bonita,* I show you some moves you never forget.'

Andrews stomped his left foot, hard, and he reeled back, his face contorted in agony and rage, spat:

'Cunt . . . *puta,* you are a lesbian, no?'

Roberts was back and seeing Caz's pain, smiled, said:

'I see you guys hit it off.'

Andrews said:

'I showed *him* some moves.'

Roberts liked it, a lot, said:

'Let's move. See if Mr Dunne is currently available.'

Caz, massaging his left foot, demanded:

'What about my money?'

Roberts was already moving, said:

'Cheque's already in the mail.'

Caz swore for the hundredth time. He was definitely getting into a new line of work, and the *puta,* he'd find a way to settle with her. Roberts he couldn't touch but her, the bitch, what was she? A constable . . . ha . . . a nothing and he felt better at the various ways he could fuck with her.

Outside, Roberts stood for a moment, watching the traffic till Andrews went:

'Sir?'

Ammunition

It was like he'd forgotten she was there, he said:

'What?'

She was anxious to get moving, get this Terry Dunne before the word got out. They brought him in, it was a career maker, a white arrest in fact. The mythical Holy Grail of policework, the case that made you golden. She said:

'Shouldn't we be moving, get this Terry Dunne before he goes to ground.'

Roberts shoulders slumped, he said:

'Oh our Mr Dunne isn't going anywhere.'

She was surprised, asked:

'You know where he is?'

She was beginning to understand why Roberts was a chief inspector. He looked at her, said:

'He's in the morgue.'

She didn't know what to make of that and Roberts, seeing her confusion, said:

'He was found on Canary Wharf, three bullets in the gut, two in the head.'

Was the case over then she wondered and, as if reading her mind, Roberts said:

'It means he fucked up so they terminated his employment, next time, it will a more serious effort.'

She echoed:

'Next time.'

Roberts was heading towards the car, said:

'The next time they take a run at Brant.'

Roberts let her do the driving and seemed sunk in gloom, she asked:

'Where to now, sir?'

He didn't raise his head, said:

'Good question.'

Back at the station, Roberts told her to go the canteen, get some teas, and bring them back to his office. She was going to protest that she was a policewoman, getting tea was not her job, but felt it wouldn't be the best time to bring it up. So, with sarcasm barely concealed, she asked:

'And how would *Sir* like it?'

Without missing a beat, he said:

'Quickly.'

Seething, she was en route when the notice board caught her attention, the results of the sergeants' exams were posted and she scrolled the names, saw Falls had made it, muttered:

'That's all I need.'

She knew Falls had failed twice already and this would have been her last shot, Andrews was confident Falls would fail again. But the cow had passed. The chances of Andrews making that rank were out the window now. Two female sergeants in the same station.

Yeah, like that was ever going to happen.

The whole day was down the toilet and she was running errands, like some airhead secretary. She'd have to rethink her whole strategy, get her name back up there in lights.

The worst part was, when she ran into Falls, she was going

to have to do that whole gushing delighted gig, act like she was over the bleeding moon. She could feel bile in her throat. A passing cop said:

'The chief inspector wants to know if you're brewing the tea yourself, you'd need to show a bit more initative.'

Words failed her.

Roberts rang the hospital, got the update on Brant, not only was the sergeant sitting up but complaining. Roberts had arranged for two armed cops to be on duty at Brant's door.

Brant, on hearing the names of the two officers assigned, had said:

'Those fucks are likely to shoot me themselves.'

If he kept whining, Roberts might take a shot too. He'd put the phone down, roared:

'Where's me bloody tea?'

The phone shrilled again and he snapped up the receiver, barked:

'What?'

Heard:

'Tut, tut, Chief Inspector, is that any way to answer a call?'

The posh bastard, the one who'd called about shooting Brant, Roberts counted to ten, then said:

'Tell me you want to give yourself up.'

Heard that eerie cackle, like some crazed banshee, the guy said:

'Here I am, doing your work for you, and I don't detect . . . sorry, no pun intended, I don't sense any gratitude.'

Andrews came in, put the tea on his desk, spilling a part on his files. He glared at her and she scarpered. He returned his attention to the call, asked:

'Sorry, mate, what am I supposed to be grateful for?'

A moment's hesitation, then:

'Don't be coy, Inspector, Canary Wharf . . . ring any bells?'

Roberts decided to go with it, said:

'We discovered the body of a man there, so?'

A sound of irritation, then:

'Don't play silly buggers with me, Inspector, I'm trying to keep you in . . . how do they term it . . . ah yes, in the loop, but you're trying my patience.'

Roberts felt a small victory. He'd annoyed the bastard, get him angry, he'd got careless. He said:

'Are you telling me the man we found is connected to the shooting of Sergeant Brant?'

The guy's voice had upped an octave, and he said:

'Very good, Inspector. Yes, he was the shooter, if a rather poor one, so I felt it best to terminate his contract.'

Roberts chanced a gulp of tea, it burned like a mother, made him near retch and . . . no fucking sugar. He'd have Andrews's arse, he asked:

'You're telling me you killed him, is that what you're saying?'

Ammunition

'Bravo, Inspector, you're finally on the same page.'

This was one of those expressions that got up Roberts's nose, nearly as bad as . . . *singing from the same hymn sheet.*

Roberts asked:

'And now, where we do go from here?'

Another chuckle and the guy said.

'You're familiar with the expression, if at first . . . ?'

Roberts felt a surge of adrenaline, asked:

'You're not seriously going to try again?'

As he said it, the voice said:

'See, we're singing from the same hymn sheet.'

Click.

He was gone.

The cops don't want anybody to have guns except them—I wonder why?
—Eddie Bunker

10

McDONALD PREPARED FOR his meet with the old-age vigilantes, that's how he thought of them, get a pension and get armed. He wore a black track suit, put a knit cap in his pocket, pulled on a black windbreaker, and in the side pocket, slipped his Walther PKK.

This weapon he'd taken off a drug dealer in Brixton. It gave him a sense of power that continued to amaze him. He'd stood in front of the mirror, the weapon in his right hand, hanging loosely by his side, casual but lethal, a half smile on his face, asking his reflection:

'You wanna fuck with me? Huh, that what you want?'

Why it came out in an American accent was not something he analysed. It just seemed to run with the deal. It felt . . . fitting. He'd levelled the gun at his reflection on many nights when he'd overindulged in the marching powder, thinking of the coke.

Man, that shit sneaks up on you, you start, like what, the odd line? Then a few more at the weekend, you know, ease the brewskis along, then fuck, next thing Monday mornings, you wake, you are brewing coffee, hopping in the shower, popping bread in the toaster.

Are you, fuck?

You're on your knees on the carpet, scraping up dust and hopefully remnants of cocaine and the damn question of course, *You got a little Jones going here, fellah?* Naw, course not, so your nose streamed a bit, it was fucking England, damp weather, what'd you expect?

Lately, he'd cut back on the old nose candy, got himself up to speed, in the real sense, scored some amphetamines, now those babes, they kept you sharp, kept you in the game and man, he so wanted to be a player, and if they wouldn't let him be a force *in the Force,* then fuck 'em, he'd get his own followers. So, they were old, you can't get it all.

He put a few tabs of the speed in his trouser pocket and, yeah, he was ready to roll. He saluted himself in the mirror, said:

'Let's go *dispense* some frontier justice.'

He got the tube to Balham. The old codger had a council house just down from the station. He came out of the station and the minute he hit the street, he could feel the vibe, not exactly drums beating but the blood in the wind, the simmering violence in the air. He smiled, it was gonna be a good one. On his way to the house, two different guys gave him the hard stare, the granite-eyed question:

'The fuck you looking at?'

He loved it, the dope cruising in his veins, the Walther

snug in his jacket. He began to hum the theme from *The So-pranos.*

His fervour faltered a little when he got into the house and old Bill introduced him to the crew. Jesus, how old were they?

Four of them, none under seventy. Bill said:

'Meet the gang.'

McDonald snapped:

'No names, this is a professional gig.'

Got their attention.

Already, from the street, he could hear the shouts, yahoos of the coming evening. One of the men looked nervously towards the window, and Bill said:

'It's early yet, they're just warming up, come midnight they'll be in full roar.'

McDonald said nothing for a moment, then asked:

'You get everything?'

Bill, anxious to please, went to get the equipment and one of the guys asked McDonald:

'You're a copper?'

He had an edge, an accusation to his question.

McDonald said:

'I'm *your* best hope is what I am.'

A guy wearing a tartan scarf asked:

'What do you think we can do, they're running riot out there?'

McDonald said:

'We're going to reclaim a tiny part of Great Britain.'

Ammunition

They stared at him with scepticism and he said:

'First we take back this street and then who knows.'

Bill arrived back, with a bin liner, emptied the contents on the carpet, out tumbled baseball bats, balaclavas, cricket bats, and one lethal-looking hammer.

McDonald said:

'Okay, let's get primed.'

He doled out the various items and the men seemed unsure as they hefted the various weapons. McDonald asked:

'Is there a key figure in the gangs?'

Bill said:

'A West Indian kid, about twenty, he seems to control most of the activity. He's always surrounded by four or five dangerous-looking guys, one black and three white guys.'

He sounded horrified that white men would be part of such mayhem. McDonald asked:

'He got a name?'

One of the others said:

'They call him "Trick".'

McDonald smiled, said:

'Trick or treat.'

He checked his watch, looked at Bill, said:

'We have some time, how about some refreshments while I lay out the plan of action.'

Bill had sherry, some cider, and a bottle of gin that looked like it had been there since the Second World War. Bill dispensed mugs and McDonald did the host bit, poured gener-

66

ous amounts of each beverage to his crew. He had a large gin himself, said:

'Now listen up, this is not going to be pretty, once we get out there, you do exactly like I'm about to tell you. If you have any qualms, get to fuck home now.'

He waited, saw some nervous glances, but they stayed put, he said:

'Good, now here's how it's going to go down.'

When he'd finished, one of the men, sipping sherry, asked:

'Isn't that a tad . . . drastic?'

McDonald walked over to him, stopped, then lashed out, knocking the mug across the room, said:

'Don't ever . . . ever question me. You want to live in fear, huddled under the sheets, or do you want to be a man?'

There was a stunned silence, then Bill said:

'We're with you, Boss.'

McDonald liked that, liked it a lot.

The four old men, McDonald watched them as the time ticked away and the noise from the street intensified. There was the guy in the tartan scarf who seemed gung ho, especially after the pint of cider. Next, was a guy with thick glasses, and McDonald tagged him as the owl. He might be useful if he could actually see anything. Bill, of course, and sitting beside him was a solid-looking man, who might have been a docker in his day. McDonald reckoned he'd be fine.

Then was there the librarian, you just knew he'd never swung anything more wieldly than a book.

McDonald went through the strategy again, insisting they not waver from this, the whole fuel being . . . fast and dirty.

He popped a tab of speed and told them to suit up. In the balaclavas, dark clothing, they seemed a touch more formidable but not really up to close scrutiny. He nodded and as they moved to the back door, the librarian halted, said: 'I can't . . . I can't go out there.'

McDonald wanted to knock him on his arse, the whole deal could fold right there, he said:

'Okay, that's fine. You go and gather up some serious booze, you can be the provisions officer. We'll need fortifying.'

And then they were moving along the back garden, McDonald held a thick length of pipe in his hand, they came round the street, McDonald in the lead, the four close behind.

Gathered round a minivan were a loud, boisterous group. The centre was a small guy in his twenties, swigging from a bottle of vodka, giving it large. Trick

As arranged, they waded in immediately, swinging bats, hammer, and not uttering a sound. They felled most of the gang in the initial assault, and McDonald was cheered to see the docker give a few extra kicks to the guy he'd dropped. Then McDonald was in front of Trick, whose jaw had literally dropped, he gasped:

'The fuck is this?' McDonald swung the pipe, crushing the guy's lower jaw, and kicked him in the balls as his head snapped back, McDonald knelt by him, grabbed his hair, twisted, said:

'You ever appear in this street again, we'll kill you and everyone belonging to you.'

He heard a groan behind him, Bill had taken a knife in the gut, the knife holder was standing now, professional stance, his mouth leaking blood, he glared at them, growled:

'C'mon, you wankers, who's next . . . ?'

They'd had the initial advantage of surprise and had done really well but it all hung in the balance, a moment when all could go down the toilet, and he could sense his crew on the verge of flight.

He shot the knife holder, in both knees, said:

'Troops disengage.'

He had to drag Bill along, blood seeping from his stomach, the docker grabbed his other arm and they were down the street, circled behind the houses and back thorough the gardens. McDonald could hear the wail of sirens. It struck him that for the first time in his career, that sound was the enemy. They were back inside the house, the librarian waiting, his face chalky white. McDonald ordered:

'Hit the lights, we'll stay in the kitchen.'

There were three bottles of Glenfiddich on the kitchen table, McDonald got Bill onto a chair, let his head rest on the table, and grabbed a bottle, tore the seal off it, drank deep, passed the bottle to the docker, and then examined Bill's wound. It was nasty, and Bill had gone into shock. McDonald grabbed another bottle, got the top off, and poured the whisky on the gash, Bill howled in anguish, McDonald commanded:

'Get me something to bind this.'

He was handed a pile of bandages and some towels and sweat pouring off him, he managed to bind the wound. The docker said:

'He'll need hospitalization.'

McDonald nodded, said:

'Give me five minutes to get clear, then call an ambulance, say he was a victim of a mugging. Get the gear stashed away. The rest of you go home, I'll be in touch.' They stood for a moment, staring at him, and he said:

'You did good.'

He took another swig of the bottle and took off through the back garden. He dumped his balaclava in a bin, kept to the back streets moving fast and, on the edge of Clapham, hailed a cab, got in the back, and he was out of there. The driver, smoking a joint, had the radio on, loud. McDonald settled back in his seat, as Dire Straits sang. . . . 'The Sultans of Swing.'

A wide grin began to move across McDonald's face. He watched the streets as the cab sped on, groups of people everywhere and he thought:

Man, my work has just begun.

Foley, the desk sergeant, got the call about a shooting and mini-riot, and asked:

'What else is new?'

Friday night, the animals were out to play, he his copy of 'Heat,' three bacon and tomato sandwiches, a flask of tea. He settled himself in his chair, put his feet up, thought:

Ah, this is the life.

He loved the weekend, they wouldn't be dragging the scum in until about three/four in the morning, so he had a good two hours of reading and at least a half hour of kip.

Back home, McDonald was in the bath, his head back, Thin Lizzy booming from the speakers, a glass of Scotch on the rim of the bath, and he thought about Dad's army . . . thought, with deep satisfaction:

Didn't they do fucking great.

Trick, meanwhile, was having his jaw wired and that, plus the kick in the balls, had deprived him of speech, not that he had a whole lot to say, except perhaps:

'Fuck me.'

The knife wielder was having one of his legs amputated.

In another hospital, not a mile away, Bill suffered a massive coronary and was dead in twenty minutes.

The docker began to weep.

HAPPY SLAPPERS

A NEW PHENOMENON HAD swept the country . . . happy slapping. Young people strode up to an unsuspecting individual, slapped them harshly across the face, and used their mobile phone camera to instantly sent the shocked reaction to all their friends. It had mutated to extreme forms, one case where a teenage girl was photographed as she was raped. In its lesser form, members of the public, usually single women, were approached by a young person and, out of the blue, walloped into the face as the camera recorded and transmitted instantly their reaction to the assailant's mates.

It was becoming a national pastime.

After the terrible bombings in London, it actually increased, photos of victims, their faces covered in blood, were snapped by youngsters on the prowl. The tabloids loved it, displaying shocked outrage, of course, but it was the sort of story they couldn't invent and there was no indication of it abating. Psychologists, sociologists, et al. wrung their collective hands and said it was a sign of the corrosion of society and one more stage in the total breakdown of moral values.

Ammunition

A teenage boy, arrested after he'd happy slapped a woman in her seventies.

Asked why he did it, said:

' 'Cos it like, you know, rocks.'

11

FALLS APPEARED FOR duty with her stripes proudly displayed on her arm, she tried to appear cool with it, but a shit-eating grin threatened to engulf her features at any time. The other cops, grudgingly went:

'Sarge.'

The term like bile in their respective throats. She was summoned to Brown's office. She was confident the Super had a little congratulatory speech prepared, the first black female sergeant! She thought to herself:

It's been a long time coming.

And she resolved to be suitably humble and, what was the term, yeah, self-effacing.

She knocked on the door, her sense of anticipation at its zenith. She was taken aback to see PC Lane there, the fuck was he doing at her moment? Lane was the lamest cop on the force, so bland he could only be described as beige. He'd had one moment of glory when he was photographed with Tony Blair, but old Tony had lost a lot of kudos since then. Even Lane's wife had removed the framed photo from their mantelpiece, replaced it with the Dalai-lama, always a safe bet. He never said nowt, and people were vague as what exactly he ever did. The Super was huddled over papers, took five minutes before looking up, and when finally he did, he said:

'Ah, Falls, you're late.'

No Sergeant.

He leant back, addressed her, and Lane, asked:

'Are you familiar with the happy-slapping scandal?'

Falls wanted to shout:

'You pompous prick, it's in the papers every bloody day.'

She conceded she was and Lane simply nodded. The Super said:

'Good, then you know what's involved. Now I don't give a toss what they do in the rest of the country but not on my patch, do you understand?'

Falls couldn't believe it, this was the plum assignment, she tried for control, asked:

'And, sir, what is it you wish us to do?'

Brown's face clouded, he caught the tone, barked:

'Kennington seems to be the most popular site for the little bastards, get down there, stamp it out.'

Falls waited for more and the Super said:

'I'm assigning PC Lane to accompany you. He has teenagers so he knows how they think, if anyone on the damn planet can ever be said to know that.'

The fact that Lane's kids were grown adults was not something Lane mentioned.

Falls asked:

'Is that all . . . *sir?*'

Brown was back in his papers, said:

'Tell my secretary to bring my tea, and to make sure the biscuits are fresh, they were stale yesterday.'

And they were dismissed. There was no sign of his secretary and Lane, worried, asked:

'Should we try and find her?'

Falls gave him her most withering look, said:

'Take a wild fucking guess?'

For the next week, they covered the Kennington Road, with Falls sitting in the car and Lane on foot patrol. You're the sergeant, you're going to walk the beat with a constable?

Lane wasn't happy, but he didn't have a whole lot of choice and the odd times he did get to spend with Falls, she was so crabby, irritable, he was relieved to get back on solo patrol. They didn't find any Happy Slappers but did grab two pickpockets, warned off the inevitable hookers, and were mainly bored out of their minds.

Lane, used to dull assignments, took it as more of the same, but Falls was seething. She went to see Brant, and he was on the verge of being discharged, sitting up in bed, reading a porn magazine. Most guys, sneaking a peek at one of these, if someone enters the room, they try and hide it, but Brant, he lay it open at its provocative page. Falls asked:

'How do the nurses like your choice of reading?'

He looked almost the same as before, except his face was

visibly thinner and his skin a greyish pale. His spirit, that seemed as lethal as ever, he said:

'The nurses gave it to me.'

He stared at her sergeant's stripes, said:

'Welcome to the club.'

She suddenly felt slightly ashamed of them, Brant knew she'd gotten them under false pretences. As if reading her mind, he said:

'Don't sweat how you got them, just be sure to make full use of the rank.'

She blurted out about her current assignment, and he gave his demonic smile, said:

'You know why Brown is so gung ho to grab one of these slappers?'

She repeated the speech the Super had given them and he snorted, said:

'Bollocks, his wife was a victim.'

She was going to ask him how he knew, but then information was his currency.

He said:

'Those guys on the door, protecting me, bum a cig off one of them, the fat fuck, he has a pack of Embassy.'

She said:

'Isn't smoking forbidden?'

And got the look.

He said:

Ken Bruen

'Hon, when you're a wounded cop, you can do what the fuck you like.'

She opened the door and, sure enough, one of the cops was fat and did have the cigs. He handed them over with:

'Any chance he might buy his own?'

Falls nearly laughed, said:

'Why don't you ask him yourself?'

As Brant created a cloud of smoke above his head, Falls filled him in on the discovery of the dead body, the guy who'd shot Brant, and the subsequent call to Roberts. Brant listened without comment and Falls finally asked:

'Aren't you worried about the next attempt?'

He dropped the cig on the floor, said:

'Put your sergeant's heel on that, there's a good girl.'

She picked it up, extinguished it in a glass of water, then, on consideration, put the soggy thing in her jacket. Brant was highly amused, said:

'Come back this evening, you can do a clean sweep.'

And immediately lit another. He had a way of constantly irritating a person and once he knew you were fucked, he never let up. And despite all that, there was no better guy to have in your corner. She repeated her question, and he said:

'I hope he takes a shot at me sooner rather than later.'

Anyone else, you'd call it bravado. He said:

'You want off this shite detail you're on?'

She said of course, but there hadn't been a single instance. Brant shook his head, said:

'Christ, no wonder you could never pass the exam.'

She winced, and he let that hover, then said:

'Get hold of a mobile phone, with the camera on it, then grab the first fuck you see. Bring him in.'

She stared at him, asked:

'You mean plant it on a person?'

He laughed, the one that had no relation to warmth or indeed humour, said:

'Well, he's hardly going to plant it on himself.'

She hated to admit it to herself, but she'd do nigh anything to get off the assignment, asked:

'What about Lane?'

This time, he dropped the butt in the glass of water, it made a soft plink. He said:

'Lane could give a fuck. How do you think he's put in eighteen years and never made noise? You're the sergeant, you tell him what's happened, after you nick the culprit.'

She was beginning to like the sound of the set-up and asked:

'But the guy, whoever we choose, won't he claim it's a set-up?'

Brant smiled.

'Don't they all.'

Before she left, she asked:

'How are you feeling in yourself, they say a . . . a shooting can take a long time to recover from. You could take early retirement?'

For once, he actually showed some emotion, surprise principally, asked:

'And do what, become a Happy Slapper? This is the only gig I know.'

She was as the door, then said:

'Porter saved your life, you know that? He covered you with his body.'

Brant wasn't comfortable, said:

'He's a fag, any chance to jump on my bones.'

She'd finally gotten a chance at Brant, took it, said as she closed the door:

'You owe him, big time.'

The fat guard called after her:

'Hey, where's me cigarettes?'

Without turning, she said:

'He put them in water, they look lovely, real decorative.'

She went to a phone warehouse, bought the cheapest model she could find, then outside Kennington Tube Station she handed the phone to Lane, said:

'Get my pic.'

She adopted an expression of shock, like she'd just been slapped.

Two hours later, she selected her target, a guy in his twenties, walking with a swagger, elbowing people aside as he strutted towards the station. Falls said:

Ammunition

'There's our Happy Slapper. You just saw him slap me and here's his phone.'

Lane didn't say anything, just took the phone, Falls got out of the car and deliberately collided with the guy. She made it look like he'd attacked her, and began to scream blue murder. Lane was out of the car, and despite whatever reservations he'd felt, he went full into the scenario, producing the phone camera, saying loudly:

'He photographed the attack!'

His tone a mix of outrage and disbelief, three pedestrians bought what they thought they were witnessing and grabbed the young man, throwing punches at him, going:

'You animal.'

A woman helped Falls to her feet, said:

'The pig actually photographed you!'

Falls was astonished at how well it had gone, and Lane's participation added the nice touch of reality.

The young guy, named John Coleman, was too flabbergasted to speak, plus he was hurting from the punches he'd received from the witnesses. Lane arrested him, cuffed him, and shoved him in the car, Falls took the names and addresses of the pedestrians, who were more than willing to help.

Since the attacks on London, people were more than keen to get involved. Bombs were one thing, but that you couldn't walk down the street without getting a slap in the face and . . . being photographed while it happened, it was just too much outrage.

Falls got back in the car, letting Lane drive, she was shaking from the physical tussle and the sheer andrenaline of the encounter.

Lane put the car in gear, and Falls glanced back at the Happy Slapper. He seemed to be in a daze. Falls said:

'That will teach you to push people around.'

He looked up, his face a riot of confusion, said:

'But I don't even have a mobile.'

Falls held up the phone, asked:

'And what do you think this is?'

Lane gave an odd sound, as if he had something nasty in his mouth. He felt Falls was really pushing the envelope on this one. The young man tried:

'It's not my phone, you can't make this stick.'

Falls held up a sheet of paper with the witnesses names, said:

'We've enough ammunition here to put you away for two years, if you're lucky.'

She turned back to Lane, said:

'You did good.'

He was maneuvering into a space outside the station, took a moment, said:

'Not how I'd term it myself.'

Falls decided not to pursue it.

12

COLEMAN WAS CHARGED with happy slapping, termed . . . an attack on the private rights of an individual . . . incitement to public disorder and . . . more serious, an assault on a police officer. They threw in resisting arrest to round it off.

A solicitor was called and three hours later, Coleman was released on bail, due to appear in magistrates' court in a month. His brief said:

'You'll have to do jail time, I might be able to plea bargain that you didn't realize the woman was a cop, but I won't lie to you, they're keen to make an example of a Happy Slapper, you'll have to serve at least a year.'

Coleman, still in shock, made his way out of the station, to the taunts of various cops, who shouted:

'Smile, you're on *Candid Camera*.'

He ran into Falls on the steps, asked:

'Why . . . why are you doing this to me?'

Falls, feeling like Brant was speaking for her, said:

'Because I can.'

Ammunition

Coleman stared at her for a minute, resolving to get this bitch, one way or another. He stumbled down the steps, feeling like he might pass out, his whole life had gone down the toilet. He looked back at Falls. said:

'It's me twenty-first birthday today.'

She gave him a wide-eyed look, said:

'Say cheese.'

He did what you do when you're suddenly fucked out of the blue, when your whole life has turned on sixpence, he went to the pub. He grabbed a stool at the counter, and for the life of him couldn't get his mind into gear. He wanted a drink but didn't know what to order. A woman took the stool beside him, said:

'Can't decide, huh?'

He looked at her, a gorgeous blonde, lovely face with very striking eyes. She added:

'You poor lamb, you've had a terrible ordeal. Let me order for us.'

Her stress on *us* gave it a sultry sound, and to his amazement, he got a hard-on, put it down to shock. His frigging body didn't know what was going on. The barman was all over her, leching openly at her full cleavage, lust reddning his cheeks, he drawled:

'What will it be, darling?'

She rubbed her scarlet lips with her tongue, said:

'Two large gins, with slim-line tonics. A girl has to watch her figure.'

The barman glanced at the young man who seemed to be totally zoned, said:

'You got it, babe.'

She said:

'And something for your own self, how would that be?'

That would be fucking hunky-dory.

Coleman had a hundred questions, but she cut him off, said:

'Drink-ees first, then we'll nice have a chat.'

He was happy to do that, asked:

'Can I know your name?'

She gave a beautiful smile, said:

'Sweetie, you can have whatever you want. . . . I'm Angie.'

The best way to kill a man is not to confide in anybody.
—Danny Ahearn, New York mobster

13

FALLS WAS SUMMONED to the Super's office and, alas, at the time when he was taking his morning tea. This was a ritual, legendary in the station. Because of the biscuits, Rich Tea, his habit of dunking them in the cup, then slurping the soggy portion into his mouth was a test of endurance for any sane person. He was mid-slurp when Falls entered, he said:

'Have a seat, Sergeant.'

Crumbs littered his shirt and she resolved not to hear the sounds he'd make. Instead, she focused on his use of . . . 'Sergeant.' Good sign. He gave her a wide smile, not a pretty sight. With particles staining his teeth, he said:

'Fine work on that Happy-Slapper case, I intended pairing you and Lane together again, but he has requested a pairing with somebody else.'

He waited, drank some tea or rather gaggled it, Falls said nothing, and then he asked:

'Was there a problem with him?'

She said:

'He doesn't like women.'

The Super considered this and said:

'He's an old-fashioned cop, taking orders from a woman would be very difficult for him, his type of copper. They're on their way out.'

Falls wanted to say, *Pity they wouldn't take the Super with them*. She nodded at the apparent wisdom of his insight. He drained the last of his tea, belched, said:

'I'm putting you with Andrews, she could learn a lot from an old pro like you.'

He leaned on the word *pro,* letting the slur linger. Then he surprised her by asking:

'How much influence have you got with our Sergeant Brant?'

She told the truth, said:

'I don't think anyone has much sway over him.'

He frowned, then:

'I hear he's coming back and you know, a smart resourceful person like you, if you saw a way to persuade him to resign, the sky would be the limit in your own career.'

Translate as:

Help me shaft the bastard.

Falls said she would do what she could, and the Super beamed, said:

'That's my girl. I felt I could rely on you, I see you and I doing great things.'

Appointing her his new hatchet person, she knew what

had happened to McDonald, but she was smart enough to play along. She said:

'I'll give it my full attention, sir.'

Thinking:

Like fuck I will.

She was dismissed with more praise ringing in her ears. She walked straight into Roberts, who said:

'I believe you're the new golden girl.'

She and Roberts had a varied and complicated history, having each seen the other at their lowest ebb, they weren't so much friends as uneasy allies. She asked:

'Do I look delighted?'

Roberts gave her his slow look, then said:

'What you ought to do is look over your shoulder, often, and very carefully.'

Gee, like this was something she didn't know.

She found Lane in the canteen, an uneaten sandwich before him and a glass of milk, she didn't ask if she could join him, just sat down opposite him, demanded:

'What's your fucking problem?'

He stared at her, said:

'I rang a check on our Mr Coleman and, guess what, he's clean. Never been in trouble in his life, and just finished a course in computer studies.'

Falls didn't like the sound of this, not one bit, snapped:

'Hey, you saw him swaggering down the street, bumping into people.'

Ammunition

Lane pushed his sandwich away, the end of the bread had curled up. Like a bad rumour, he said:

'He's an intense young man, perhaps he was just preoccupied.'

Falls gave a bitter laugh, one that Brant would have been proud of, said:

'Well, he certainly has plenty to be preoccupied about now.'

Lane looked at her, his eyes a watery blue, like denim on its last legs, said:

'It's his birthday today.'

Boy, she was finding Lane a real pain in the arse, asked:

'Whose birthday?'

Lane let out a long sigh, like a wounded animal, said:

'Our suspect, he's twenty-one today.'

Falls knew it was time to lay weight, said:

'The Super is happy, the media will be delighted, we look good, we're off that shitty detail, everybody wins.'

Lane was shaking his head:

'That young man doesn't.'

Falls had had enough of his whining, said:

'Shit happens. He'll get what, a slap on the wrist, maybe a nominal fine, and he'll be a law-abiding citizen for the rest for his life. We've actually put him on the right road.'

Lane was now wringing his hands. She noticed his fingernails were bitten to the quick, he said:

'Sergeant, you know that's not going to happen, they'll

make an example of him, the press want it, the Super will demand it, that kid is looking at least two years.'

Falls stood up, warned:

'You're not thinking of doing anything stupid, are you, that would be a really bad move?'

Lane said, more to himself:

'You know, I haven't led a very distinguished career, but I've never done anything I couldn't sleep about, I don't want to end my time with that ruined life on my conscience.'

Falls put her face right in his, said:

'Don't fuck with me, Lane.'

And she got out of there. She was worried. If Lane came clean, not only would she lose her new stripes, she'd be thrown off the force and probably arrested. She was fucked if she'd let that happen. She'd need to see Brant and soon.

Roberts was in the corridor, summoned her, said:

'Come into my office, we have a situation.'

Jesus, she thought, *what now?*

Roberts sat behind his desk, moved all his papers aside, said:

'Last Friday night, in Balham, a group of vigilantes put some local hard cases in the hospital, shot one in the knees, broke the jaw of the ringleader.'

Falls, like most cops, secretly admired vigilante justice. It got the job done and reached the untouchables. She'd been on the fringes of the same justice herself and more than once. She knew for a fact that Brant frequently operated in such a manner.

Ammunition

She said:

'So, we have one less gang of thugs to worry about.'

Roberts gave a grim smile, said:

'Normally I'd agree with you, but one of the vigilantes got knifed, died of a subsequent heart attack. The man who brought him to the hospital was detained by a cop from Balham.'

Falls couldn't see the problem. So one of the vigilantes bought the farm, as the Yanks say, so what. They were thousands of pissed-off citizens out there more than ready to pick up the cause.

Roberts wasn't finished, continued:

'The dead guy, get this . . . he was seventy-five years old. . . .'

Falls laughed, said:

'Pensioners kicking arse, it's a new twist.'

Roberts was staring out the window, said:

'His mate, the one who was detained, he had a fairly intriguing allegation.'

Falls couldn't wait to hear it, said:

'I can't wait to hear it.'

Roberts turned round to face her, said:

'He alleges that they were organized and led by . . . a cop.'

Took her a moment to digest this, then she said:

'That's impossible.'

Roberts expression suggested it was highly possible, he said:

'I want you and Andrews to investigate this. If the press

get wind of it, they'll hang us out to dry. Go and see this guy who'd made the allegation and whatever it takes, make it go away, you understand me?'

She stood up, said:

'Yes sir.'

She was at the door when he said:

'Liz, be discreet.'

Using her first name showed the strain he was under and just how seriously he was taking this. Before tackling this, she had a call to make, Angie's solicitor, an aggressive cop hater, would be the one to tell her about Angie and, with any luck, maybe even where she was staying.

She found Andrews in the gym, working out, of course, doing the heavy weights, building up the muscle. Falls said:

'We have an assignment, of a rather sensitive nature. Pick me up in The Elephant and Castle in two hours.'

She didn't wait for a reply.

Ellen Dunne, the darling of the Left and the scourge of the Met, had her offices in The Elephant and Castle. She was highly successful and could easily have moved to more impressive locations, but she knew it was good for her image to be in the war zone, kept her cred up to speed. Her secretary, who looked like a bull dyke, treated Falls with barely concealed hostility and said Ellen was busy. Falls knew the dance, the moves, said:

'She's too busy to see a black woman?'

The woman glared at her, rang through, and then:

'She'll give you five minutes.'

Falls gave her her best smile and said:

'And you'll be timing me, am I right?'

The secretary grunted.

'Ellen Dunne had aged. The last time Falls had seen her was at Angie's trial. Now, her hair was grey, lines ran down the sides of her cheeks, and her clothes seemed slept in. Falls figured, if you spent your life defending scumbags, it rubbed off. She sat behind a large desk, piled with papers, a cigarette burning in a flowing ashtray. She watched Falls approach, said:

'You're here to make my day, right?'

Falls liked Ellen, though she continually harassed the cops, made their lives hell, she had a basic integrity that was appealing. Falls said:

'You look like shit.'

Ellen nearly smiled, she knew the crap Falls took as a woman and a black woman in the force. She countered:

'You're trying to get on my good side I think, so, what can I can I do for you . . . , Sergeant. Who'd you have to fuck for that promotion?'

Falls let that slide, asked:

'Angie, your client, she's out.'

Ellen's face clouded over, and Falls thought she spotted a shadow of . . . fear? Ellen lit a fresh cigarette, the old one still burning, wiped a hand across her eyes, said:

'She certainly is.'

Falls realized the woman was on the verge of some kind of breakdown, pressed:

'How'd that happen? I thought she was gone for good.'

Ellen let out a long sigh, said:

'She became a whiz kid on the law, so many of them do, they've nothing else to do, I suppose . . . and she discovered a discrepancy in my defence of her, was able to show I hadn't given her the full extent of my renowned talent . . . bingo, she got an appeal, and I don't have to tell you what a charmer she is . . . she had the new judge eating out of her hand, she got out two weeks ago.'

Falls was horrified, said:

'But she killed at least three people that we know of.'

Ellen sat back, weariness all over her, said:

'I've been practising for twenty years and met every kind of animal you can imagine, and yes, I defended them, with all my energy. But Angie, she was the first one to ever scare me. When I went to defend her, I made sure she'd be found guilty. It never cost me a night's sleep, there are the rare ones like her, who should never see the light of day.'

Falls asked:

'Do you know where she is?'

Ellen shook her head, then:

'She phoned me, said she'd be round to settle my account.'

Then she looked at Falls, said:

'I'm guessing you've heard from her too.'

Ammunition

Falls didn't bother to deny it, asked:

'Do you want me to arrange some protection for you?'

Ellen smiled, a sad resigned one, said:

'Having cops around me, real bad for business.'

Falls took out a pen, some paper, said:

'Here's my number. You want help, I'm there.'

Ellen didn't bother to take the paper, said:

'You watch your own back, she might decide to see you first.'

Falls felt a flash of rage. She hated to see this spirited woman so crushed, near shouted:

'I'm not afraid of her.'

Ellen had already dismissed her, her head back among the pile of files, and Falls was at the door when Ellen added:

'You should be.'

Andrews was parked at The Elephant and Castle and Falls got in, said:

'Drive to Balham.'

Andrews could tell from Falls's face that she was not exactly in a sunny disposition, but asked:

'What's our assignment?'

Falls was silent for a full minutes, then said:

'A rogue cop.'

Andrews didn't want to push, so said:

'That's not good.'

Falls spat:

'It's fucked is what it is.'

I am here to fight feminism.
—Marc Lepine, before he massacred fourteen female
students at Montreal University

14

PORTER NASH HAD been going through Brant's cases, trying to find who might have the most cause to actually take out a contract on him. It had to be serious if you were to risk offing a cop. Thing was, almost every single case, with Brant's unique style of policing, gave rise to a suspect. It was fast becoming . . . *who wouldn't want to shoot him?*

Jesus, Porter had wanted to take a pop himself.

These files were, of course, only the official ones, 90 per cent of Brant's activities were . . . as they say . . . off the books. He wasn't exactly the type of cop who wrote up a report on his actions. His spectre loomed large over South-East London. There wasn't a villain, snitch, or hooker who didn't know of him or about him. The two people who probably knew him best, if anyone ever knew him, were Roberts and Falls, and they were saying very little. Falls when Porter had approached her, snapped:

'What, you working for Internal Affairs now?'

Shut that right down.

And Roberts, his reply:

Ammunition

'Are you questioning me?'

Real big help.

But with the scant data at his disposal, Porter could already put some names on the list. One, a Spanish woman who'd tried to poison Brant and got eight years for her troubles. She was now out and present whereabouts . . . unknown. Second, the legendary top villain, Bill, who'd more or less run the South-East till Brant closed him down. Like most *retired* villains, he was living it large on the Costa del Sol. Easy enough to arrange a hit from sunny Spain, all you needed was the cash. The actual shooter, Terry Dunne, was simply a gun for hire. Porter checked his file, he had lived with his girlfriend in Clapham, Porter noted the address, figured it wouldn't hurt to pay her a visit, see if she knew who contracted her late lover. Third, and here, Porter's interest grew, The Case of the Clapham Rapist. A vicious serial rapist had been terrorizing the Clapham, Balham areas, Falls was used as a decoy, with McDonald as backup. McDonald had fucked up, and Falls had been literally pinned down by the rapist, a knife to her throat, when Brant appeared, and here's where it got murky . . . in the ensuing melee, the rapist had *fallen* on his own knife. It stank to high heaven and no investigation had followed as the public were so relieved to have the rapist off the radar.

Porter checked his name.

Barry Lewis, thirty-two years old, a short-order cook. He had one brother, Rodney, a trader in the city. Porter sat back, he'd heard the tapes of the calls made to Roberts. A posh voice, arrogant air . . . yeah, sounded like all the financial wankers Porter had the misfortune to know.

He underlined Rodney's name, and address, lived in an apartment in Mayfair, lots of cash is how that translated. Porter said aloud:

'Rodney, I must pay you a visit.'

Old Rodney certainly had the wedge to hire a shooter and, Christ, he certainly had motive. Waiting all these years made sense. Who'd believe he wouldn't have acted at the time. Porter's instincts told him this was definitely looking promising. His phone rang, and speak of the devil, it was Brant, who said:

'I'm being discharged today.'

Porter said:

'That's great, how do you feel?'

A pause as he heard Brant inhale what must have been a lethal amount of nicotine, then:

'Feel? . . . I feel fucking pissed off, when are you coming to collect me?'

Porter didn't know he'd been assigned the task, said:

'I didn't know I'd been assigned the task?'

Brant whistled, it pierced Porter's eardrum, then:

'Oh, it's a task is it?'

Porter closed the files, tried:

'I didn't mean that, I'm on my way.'

If Brant was grateful, he wasn't expressing it, said:

'Get some coffee en route. The shite they serve here isn't fit for Pakis.'

Porter sighed, he never got used to the casual racialism of his fellow officers. He asked:

'Anything else?'

Letting the sarcasm leak all over the question, Brant said:

'A slice of Danish and, mind, real coffee, none of that designer crap you pofftahs drink.'

Click.

Porter wondered for the hundredth time how on earth he managed to sustain his friendship with this . . . pig?

He ran into Roberts on his way out, said he was en route to collect Brant. Roberts gave a grim, knowing smile, asked:

'And how is he?'

'Rude as hell.'

'Ah, he's recovered then.'

When Porter arrived at the hospital, he was in a foul mood, a git had cut him in traffic and worse, given him the finger. Jesus, if he'd had time, he'd have gone after the prick, done him for every traffic violation in the manual.

His diabetes was really acting up something fierce, he was way past his check-up time, his glucose levels were through the fucking roof.

Stress, the number one enemy of insulin protection and he was under more stress than Tony Blair. Then he parked in the hospital, conscious he was way late for Brant, and a parking guy came running over, shouting:

'Hoy, you . . . the fuck do you think you're playing at?'

Porter swirled on him, the guy was small but built, and his

whole body language suggested he'd had one shit life and everybody was going to pay the freight, Porter whipped out his warrant card, said:

'You talking to me?'

The guy backed off a bit, not too much but sufficient, said:

'That space is for hospital staff, not even cops are supposed to use it.'

He had a voice that was made to whine, Porter reined in a little, asked:

'You get mugged, who you gonna call?'

The guy wasn't buying it, sneered:

'Well, not the boys in blue, that's for sure, they only look out for the rich.'

Porter nearly laughed, a damn socialist to boot, he said:

'Do yourself a favour fellah, piss off.'

The guy had more to say but decided to let it slide, went with:

'I'll let it go this time. . . .'

Porter shook his head, walked away.

He wasn't sure but the guy might have shouted:

'Arse bandit.'

Brant was resplendent in a new suit, a very expensive one, blue shirt, and the police federation tie, heavy brogue shoes, hand-made, you could tell from the stitching, but his face looked waxen, he was chatting to a nurse, scoring heavily from the look on her face. He turned to Porter, said:

'This is Mary, an Irish girl, gave me a sponge bath.'

Is there an answer to this, any reply that doesn't sound bitter? Porter asked:

'You good to go?'

Brant stood up, and Mary said:

'I'll get the wheelchair.'

Brant looked at Porter, said:

'Regulations. They have to wheel you off the premises.'

He lowered himself into the chair and when Mary went to push it, he waved her off, said:

'My officer will do it, he's built for speed.'

A not so funny joke between them. Brant had persuaded an agent to buy a book from him, the problem being, he hadn't written anything, had lured Porter to his home, spiked his coffee with speed, and jotted down Porter's war stories. The book titled *Calibre* was due for publication soon. When Porter had finally confronted Brant about literally stealing his material, Brant had shrugged:

'It's a novel, who gives a fuck.'

Porter still hadn't quite decided what he was going to do about it. He knew from bitter experience, you never won against Brant, one way or another, he'd fuck you over and sometimes, it was simply best to just bend over.

He wheeled Brant slowly till Brant snapped:

'The fuck is the matter with you, mate, push the frigging thing, stop behaving like an old woman.'

Porter debated just letting go, see what would happen, maybe the No 9 bus was due and would do them all a favour.

He finally got Brant in the car and put the vehicle in gear, burned rubber out of there.

First thing, Brant lit a cigarette, despite the decals all over the dash, commanding NO SMOKING, PLEASE!

Brant said:

'I hear you saved my life.'

Porter was stunned, of all the things he expected from the sergeant, this had never entered his radar, he shrugged, said:

'More reflex than anything else.'

If he was expecting gratitude, it wasn't coming. Brant asked:

'You figure I owe you now?'

There was a real granite edge to his words, that Mick attitude spilling all over his intonation. Porter said:

'The Chinese believe if you save a person, you're responsible for them from then on.'

He knew it sounded like a crock.

Brant stubbed his cig out on the carpet of the car, Porter nearly hit him and Brant said:

'I don't like to owe anybody, you hear me?'

Porter felt he finally, in all their tangled relationship, gotten a slight upper hand but he'd have to tread real carefully. Brant would bite at the very moment you least expected. He said:

'I might be on to the guy who ordered the hit.'

Then he ran through the names he'd jotted down, Brant listened with total concentration.

A focused Brant was a very dangerous animal.

He said:

Ammunition

'Swing the car round.'

Porter, surprised, went:

'What?'

'You deaf, turn the fucking thing around, let's go see the Clapham Rapist's brother, Rodney, is it?'

Porter swung round, a U-turn in the middle of heavy traffic, followed by howls of car horns. Brant put out his middle finger to all. Porter asked:

'Shouldn't we get some more evidence before we confront him?'

Brant snorted:

'Fuck that, I'll know if he's the cunt.'

The sheer vehemence of his words and the obscenity Porter loathed made him swerve dangerously but he reined in, pulled the car back on track, said:

'He lives in Mayfair.'

Brant was shaking his head, said:

'No good, let's go to his office, do the whole cop heavy deal, let his colleagues see who he is.'

Porter was very uneasy, intimidation, though he used it, never sat easily, and he tried:

'But what if he's innocent?'

Brant laughed, an ugly cackle, said:

'Then he's nothing to worry about, has he?'

Porter was nearing the city, the smell of money in the air, the bombings had dented the traders . . . sure . . . but not for long . . . money recovers faster than anything else on the planet.

Ask Donald Trump.

Brant leaned over, turned on the radio, and, of course, didn't ask:

'You kidding?'

The song playing was 'First Cut Is the Deepest' and to Porter's amazement, Brant listened intently, and . . . looked like he was suffering, then he snapped the radio off, asked:

'Know who wrote that song?'

Without hesitation, Porter said:

'Rod Stewart?'

Brant was delighted, said:

'Everybody thinks that. Bet you twenty quid it wasn't.'

Porter was so relieved to see him come out of the suffering mode that he agreed to the wager and asked:

'So, who do you think wrote it?'

Brant was lighting another cig and Porter would have sold his soul for a drag, Brant exhaled, said:

'I don't think, I *know* who did.'

Porter found a space near Rodney Lewis's office, prodded:

'Yeah, so is it like a secret or do we have a bet?'

Brant laughed, said:

'Fucking money from a baby, money for old rope . . . it was Cat Stevens.'

Porter felt he already had the twenty in his wallet . . . *Cat Stevens* . . . yeah, right.

Friends say I'm putting a brave face on it—Bollocks—
This is far and away the most stimulating, fascinating
thing that's ever happened to me.

—Jonathan King, songwriter, impresario, DJ, . . . jailed
for buggery

15

THE BUILDING HOUSING Rodney Lewis's office was impressive in that English mode. Let you know in an understated fashion that *here be mega bucks* and managed to convey that, unless you had lots of cash, you were way off track. Lewis's office was spacious, bright, with a severe secretary sitting behind an impressive desk. Porter had asked a few moments before:

'How'd you want to play this?'

Brant, not breaking stride, asked:

'Play what? Talk right for fuck's sake.'

Porter explained did they want to do the tried and familiar route of good cop/bad cop?

Brant said:

'Only if I get to play the good cop, I'm tired of always being the hard arse.'

Porter wanted to shout:

'How do you think we feel?'

He said:

'Okay, make a nice change.'

Ammunition

The secretary was not pleased to see them, Porter asked if they might have a word with Mr Rodney Lewis? Her expression said that pigs might fly, she snapped:

'Do you have an appointment? Mr Lewis is a very busy man.'

Porter was gearing up to be the hard arse when Brant said:

'Tell him the cops are here, in connection with his shooting of a policeman.'

She was stunned and Porter stared, mouth open at Brant, Brant said to him:

'Close your mouth, you look like a half-wit.'

The secretary went to the back of the office, disappeared behind an oak door, Brant said:

'Probably grabbing a smoke.'

Porter was furious, accused:

'What happened to our deal?'

Brant was pocketing some pens from the secretary's desk, said:

'You think that was bad? Man, that's me real mellow side.'

The secretary was back, said:

'Mr Lewis will see you now, he's the last door on the right.'

Brant winked at her and they headed for the office. Porter was about to knock, but Brant just opened the door, strode in.

Rodney Lewis had one of those ear things that lets you talk on the mobile, hands free, he was in his late forties, dressed in pinstripe, with a full head of coiffed grey hair. He was carrying plenty of weight, the kind that came from good food, and he had sharp dark eyes that watched them with a vague disinterest. What he mostly conveyed was confidence and money, oodles of both. A slight smile played on his lower lip, he asked:

'Gentlemen, to what do I owe the pleasure of the visit?'

Porter couldn't swear but he sure sounded like the guy on the tape, the rich, posh accent, with arrogance riding point. Brant slumped into a chair, on Lewis's right, Porter stayed standing. Brant asked:

'Why'd you shoot me?'

Lewis sat stock still for a moment, then recovered, reached for his phone, said directly to Porter:

'I think we better get my lawyer in on this.'

Porter looked at Brant, who, naturally, was lighting a cig, then he said:

'There's no need, sir. We were just wondering if you could perhaps help us with the shooting of a police officer?'

Lewis watched Brant for a minute, then said:

'Of course, Sergeant Brant, who was involved in the death of my brother, and you think what? That this was my revenge?'

Brant continued to say nothing, just smoked like his life depended on it, Porter tried:

'You can appreciate, sir, that we have to look at everybody who might harbour a grudge towards the sergeant.'

Lewis began to punch numbers into the phone and Porter said:

'Well, thank you for your time, sir, we'll be off now, and sorry for the inconvenience.'

Porter didn't know what Brant might do, but to his surprise and considerable relief, Brant stood up, leaned over the desk, and dropped his cig in Lewis's cup of coffee. Then they were at the door and Porter realized he was sweating, Brant turned back, asked:

'How come a fuck like you, you got all this money, you can't find somebody to shoot straight?'

Lewis locked eyes with Brant, said:

'I hope you enjoyed your little game, Sergeant. By tomorrow, I'll have your warrant card. Your days of aggression are over.'

Brant seemed like he might move back towards Lewis and Porter was ready to prevent that, Brant said:

'Your brother, the rapist, he was a piece of shit, but you, you're something even worse.'

When they were outside the building, Porter launched:

'The fuck is the matter with you? I thought we'd agreed on the good cop routine for you?'

Brant moved towards their car, said:

'That *was* my good cop. If I'd been the other, Lewis would be hitting the pavement about now.'

He looked up the building, asked:

'What is it, ten stories? He came out the window, you think that'd do it?'

Porter threw up his arms in disgust, got in the car, Brant was on his mobile phone and waited a moment, said:

'And a good afternoon to you, love your show, I was wondering if you could tell me who wrote 'First Cut'?'

He nodded, cut the connection, said:

'You owe me twenty quid.'

Porter sighed, a sigh that contained all the times that Brant had exasperated him, asked:

'What now?'

Brant said in a perfect tone of P. G. Wodehouse:

'Home, Jeeves, home.'

16

FALLS AND ANDREWS were in the home of Tim Peters, the man who said his vigilante group were led by a cop. Falls had once heard, *Never trust a man with two first names*.

The guy looked like a docker, a very elderly one, he was seventy if a day. Falls said:

'Mr Peters, if you wouldn't mind going through your story one more time, so we're sure of all the details.'

'Tim.'

Falls stopped, asked:

'What?'

He had once been a powerfully built man, but age had diminished if not deleted his physical prowess. His voice was ragged, like someone who'd smoked a thousand cigarettes and wasn't finished yet. He smiled, exposing National Health false teeth, gleaming in their whiteness. He said:

'Please call me Tim.'

They could do that, but Falls mainly wanted to call his bluff. A group of old-age vigilantes, for fuck's sake. Andrews, anxious to impress Falls, took over, said:

Ammunition

'Tim it is, now if we could have the story from the beginning?'

He took out a plastic bag and some cigarette papers, offered them, they declined, and he began to expertly roll one. He said, as he wet the rollie:

'Bill . . .'

His voice faltered, a sorrow leaking over it, then continued:

'Lord rest him, he saw a copper on the beat, outside that new shopping centre in Balham?'

Falls knew how easy it would be to see who was on duty there, and already she had a sinking feeling as to who it might be. Only one copper was pulling those shite details.

He continued:

'Bill saw him ram one of those hoodies against a wall, it sure impressed Bill. Those kids, they wear the hoods pulled up, adds to their intimidation, and they got to talking. Bill told him of the problems we were having in the street here.'

Andrews interrupted:

'Which problems were they?'

Falls shot her a look, Jesus, never interrupt a witness in full flow. He was taken aback then focused, said:

'Every weekend, they gather outside, shouting and drinking, taking God knows what drugs, that crack cocaine no doubt, playing loud, awful music, that rap stuff, and sometimes, they'll throw a brick through the window. And if you go out? Well, you didn't ever go out, too many of them, the ringleader was an Asian fellah, nicknamed Trick. He was a nasty piece of work.'

Andrews did it again, asked:

'Why didn't you call the police?'

His laugh was slightly louder than Falls's was, he said:

'Yeah, they'd rush over our area, it's a real high priority on their list.'

His bitterness was deep and set, he went on:

'So, this copper, he suggested we form a group, take them on, deal with it our own selves.'

Andrews again:

'Tim, I'm a little surprised you were so easily convinced to form what is, in reality, a criminal group?'

His shout startled her as he echoed:

'Criminal? I'll tell you what's criminal, lass, and that's to live in fear.'

Falls nearly smiled, it shut Andrews up. He said:

'It seemed like the answer to our prayers and it was going good . . .'

His face lit up as he briefly relived the rush of laying out on for the thugs. He had real energy in his voice as he said:

'The little bastards never knew what hit them, and we were winning, till Bill . . . till Bill got, well . . . you know.'

Andrews, trying to regain some ground, asked:

'Please describe the alleged policeman?'

He shook his head, said:

'No need.'

Falls was definitely warming to the guy. Andrews, a note of petulance in her voice, sat up straight, asked:

'Are you refusing to give us . . .'

He cut her off with:

'Calm down, lass. I don't need to describe him.'

Andrews, standing now, leaned over him, said:

'Sir, let me remind you that failure to cooperate with the police . . .'

He put up his hand to stop her, said:

'I have a photograph.'

Neither of the policewomen spoke. He stood up, went to a chest of drawers, said: 'My niece gave me one of them phone camera jobs, and I got a snap of him the night we went to war.'

He produced the photo. Falls was up, grabbed it out of his hand, flipped the cover, and hit the button, the photo came up and her heart sank

McDonald, in all his reckless glory, the stupid fuck. Andrews was reaching for the phone, but Falls snapped it shut, said to Tim:

'We'll need to take this into evidence.'

He was upset, asked:

'How will I call my niece?'

Falls was heading for the door, said:

'We'll see you have it back by the end of the day. Thank you for your cooperation.'

Andrews looked like she had no idea what Falls was doing but followed, Tim stood on the footpath, asked:

'Will I be on the telly?'

Falls gave him a brief look, the poor bastard, and felt a moment of pity, which she quickly suppressed. She said:

'Oh, you're going to be real famous.'

His face lit up, those white teeth gleaming in the ancient face, and she could see in that smile the man he used to be.

Andrews put the car in gear, asked:

'Back to the station?'

Falls had the phone in her hand, said:

'Drive over Lambeth Bridge.'

Andrews, proud of how well she was learning the geography of the area, said:

'There's a shorter way.'

Falls gripped her by the right arm, hissed:

'For fucking once today, do what you're told and enough with the bloody questions, you screwed up a perfectly good witness with your by-the-book routine. What the hell is the matter with you?'

Andrews wanted to go:

'Show me the photo.'

They reached the bridge and, surprisingly, traffic was light. Falls said:

'Pull up here.'

She rolled down her window, hefted the phone in her

hand, then chucked it high and wide, tilted her head as if she was waiting to hear the splash.

She didn't.

Andrew's gasped. She couldn't believe what had just happened and when she found her voice, said:

'That was evidence.'

Falls didn't look at her, simply said:

'No, that was ammunition.'

I wish I could write a book and not have to make a living.

—John W. Dean, Watergate conspirator

17

ANDREWS THOUGHT LONG and hard as to whether she should report Falls. She knew the code . . . *never rat out another cop.* You might not like your fellow officers and, right off the bat, she could bring to mind at least six she downright loathed but . . . you stuck by them. The enemy were civilians. On the other hand, Falls had treated her like shit, yeah, as if she couldn't be trusted with seeing the photo of the rogue vigilante guy.

Fuck that!

And, if Falls were reported, she'd lose her stripes, that was for damn sure, be lucky to even stay on the force and that meant a vacancy. Andrews was still relatively new, but she knew one bloody thing, the powers that be would have a white face any day of the week.

Then she told herself, all of these considerations aside, morally she was obliged to do the right thing and that was shaft Falls.

Sorry, report the suppression of evidence.

Thus, ethically uplifted, she headed for the Super's office

and was dismayed to find he was golfing. She was moving away when she almost walked into Roberts. He asked:

'What's up?'

It was now or never, so she asked if she might have a word, a private one. He said sure and led her into his office, closed the door, indicated she should sit.

She did.

He sat on the edge of the desk, told her to fire away. She gave him the whole story. His expression remained neutral, and she was pretty sure he was impressed. Such zeal as she was showing was out of the ordinary. She sat back, waiting for the heap of praise, perhaps even his backing for her nomination as acting sergeant.

He said,

'You treacherous bitch.'

For the next ten minutes he lectured her about loyalty, snitch cops and what happened to them, and wound up with:

'You want to stay being a policewoman?'

She assured him she did, and he snapped:

'Then shut your fucking mouth. Now get out of my office.'

Crushed, she was in the corridor, Porter came by, asked:

'You alright, love?'

She strode off without answering him. He knocked on Roberts door, heard:

'Come in.'

Roberts was pouring a shot of whisky into a mug, asked:

'Care to join me?'

Porter wanted to say it was a little early for him and certainly too early for a chief inspector, but the look on Robert's face stopped that. He merely shook his head and Roberts asked:

'You ever see *Serpico*?'

Porter had, anything with Pacino, he'd seen a couple of times. He said he had and Roberts asked:

'Did you agree with him, ratting out cops?'

Porter realized this was a loaded question, tried for:

'We have to stick together.'

And got the look from Roberts, the one that said:

'Are you shitting me?'

So he did the obvious, asked:

'Were you thinking of giving someone up?'

Roberts gave him a glance of such withering contempt that he felt it all the way to his backbone. Roberts said:

'I'd put a bullet in my head before I'd screw another cop.'

Porter hadn't anything to reply to this. He felt as if Roberts was testing him, see if he was the type who, given the right circumstances, would fuck over another policeman. He settled his face in what he hoped was a look of . . . *Me?* . . . *shit, I'd never give up one of our own.*

Roberts said:

'Andrews, she's got a bee in her bonnet. She might be about to shop someone.'

Porter wanted to ask who but settled for:

'She's young, she'll learn.'

Ammunition

Roberts face was a mask of restrained fury, he said:

'She fucking better.'

There was an uneasy silence and Porter was unsure where to go. Roberts asked

'What's the story with Brant?'

So Porter filled him in, gave the breakdown on their encounter with Rodney Lewis.

Roberts was smiling, not a smile of warmth or humour but the one that said it was exactly what he expected from Brant. He said:

'This Lewis, he has juice I'd say.'

Guys who worked in the city, they usually had an in with the Super: money, Freemasons, golf, all the usual old boys' network. Porter said:

'If he reports Brant and I'd imagine he will, Brant might be up the creek.'

Roberts mulled it over, said:

'Brant is always up the creek.'

No argument there.

Roberts asked:

'Your own instinct, is Lewis the guy, the one who contracted the shooting?'

Porter considered carefully. With Roberts, you committed yourself, he'd hold you to it. He said:

'He sure has motive and certainly has the cash to hire a shooter.'

Roberts went through some files, said:

'The dead shooter, Terry Dunne, he had a girlfriend. Go see her, find out what she knows, maybe she can shed some light on the deal.'

Porter thought it wasn't a bad idea, and before he could say so, Roberts snapped:

'You still here, she isn't going to come and see you, get your arse in gear.'

Porter had a lot of responses to this but none that wouldn't involve violence, he stood said:

'Right away, sir.'

And he was at the door when Roberts added:

'You see Andrews, you put her straight, got it.'

He did.

Outside, he muttered:

'Fuck.'

The American cop, Wallace was striding down the corridor, a large Starbucks in his fist. He went:

'Porter, what's up?'

Porter looked at him and, on impulse, asked:

'Want to see how we intimidate would be witnesses?'

Wallace lobbed his Styrofoam in a long wide arc and . . . slam dunk, it landed in the waste bin, he said:

'What are we waiting for, intimidation is my speciality.'

They got a car from the pool, and to Porter's disgust, only a Volvo was available. He said:

'Might as well write *Cops* on the front.'

Wallace asked if he could drive.

He could.

He made a grinding mess of the gear shift, asked:

'The fuck is the matter with you guys? Didn't you ever hear of automatics?'

Porter was amused, said:

'We heard of them, we just like to do things the hard way.'

Wallace finally got the swing of it, said:

'Yeah, I've had piss you guys call beer.'

Wallace's bulk took up most of the front seats, and Porter had to squeeze himself against the window. He asked:

'Shouldn't you be doing counterintelligence stuff?'

Wallace gave him a look, impossible to read, asked:

'What makes you think I amn't?'

18

FALLS PAID A visit to McDonald, she'd checked the duty roster, it was his day off, she got to his place early, checked the names of the apartments, he was on the ground floor, she rang his bell and smiled, thinking:

I'll be ringing his bell in more ways than one.

Her smile was grim, tinged with foreboding. She heard:

'Yeah?'

He sounded half asleep, she said:

'It's Falls, I need to speak to you.'

A pause, then:

'Can't it wait?'

She said:

'Only if you're not worried about going to jail.'

He buzzed her in.

He opened his door, cautiously, looked her over, she registered the thin white line of powder on his upper lip, thought:

Uh-oh.

He waved her in and looked down the corridor before closing the door. She asked:

Ammunition

'How paranoid are you?'

His face was the ashen grey of the habitual coke fiend, the eyes but pinpoints, his movements jerky, and the set of his body wired. She knew it from bitter experience.

He was wearing track bottoms and a T-shirt that had the logo:

THUGS GET LONELY TOO

Tupac.

She wondered if he knew that.

Then she noticed the Browning in his right hand, and chided herself, losing it. She should have spotted that right off. She asked:

'Expecting company?'

He looked at the pistol as if seeing it for the first time, said:

'They're shooting cops out there.'

The apartment was a tip, takeout food containers strewn everywhere, clothes on the floor, empty bottles lining the walls, and a smell of weed mixed with desperation. He said:

'Take a seat.'

She perched precariously on the edge of a chair. He was pacing, asked:

'Get you something?'

To buy some time, she said:

'Tea, a nice pot of tea would be good.'

He gave a crazed laugh, said:

Ken Bruen

'How fucking British is that, and you . . . black as me boots. I love it, want a nice shot of rum?'

Where did he think she was from . . . fucking Jamaica.

The gun was still in his right hand, held loosely but there. She kept her tone neutral, said:

'I'd be easier if you put the weapon away.'

He zoned out for a moment, his eyes with that lost look, and she considered taking the Browning from him. He clicked back, said:

'Tea . . . , right, won't be a mo.'

And disappeared into the kitchen. Newspapers were spread on the coffee table, to the Situations Vacant section. Ads for security personnel red lit.

She figured the only job he was getting was in the nick.

To her surprise, he returned with a tray, a clean cloth on it, and a pot of tea, two cleanish cups. He seemed more composed, and she reckoned he'd done a line . . . or two in the kitchen. He smiled, asked:

'Whasssup?'

She levelled her eyes on him, said:

'You're in a shitload of trouble.'

Didn't faze him, she knew the coke was whispering:

'No biggie.'

She gave him the whole nine, the testimony of Tim Peters, the vigilante debacle, the seriousness of a charge of inciting vigilantes, and, worse, organizing and leading them. He listened, said:

133

'They can't prove shit.'

She leaned over, said:

'You stupid prick. The guy got a photo of you.'

This got his attention, and he shouted:

'Jesus, who's seen it, where is it?'

She was tempted to let him sweat it, but he was far enough gone already. She said:

'I got it and it's at the bottom of the Thames.'

Took him a minute to digest that, then he asked:

'Why would you help me out. You've always hated me.'

Hated.

She wanted to say:

'Listen fuckhead, you'd have to get an awful lot more important for me to hate you.'

She said:

'You're a cop, I don't want to see any of our own go down.'

The coke went to another level, and he sneered:

'Mighty white of you.'

She thought she should just leave him to it, fuck him, but tried:

'You're not out of the woods yet. There's going to be an investigation, your description has been given, and the duty roster has you outside the shopping centre the day Bill said he met you.'

His face took on a scared hue, but he fronted with:

'Fuck 'em, bring it on.'

She stood up, said:

1

1

'I've covered for you, but if there's a full investigation, I don't know if anyone can save you.'

He waved her off. She knew he was already seeing the next line of coke, waiting in the kitchen, she knew that song, he said:

'Don't get your knickers in a twist, I can handle it.'

At the door she was going to offer for him to call her if he needed her but then she thought:

Screw it.

He was already in pre-coke preparation, said:

'Mind how you go, darling.'

As she got outside, she wondered if she'd been as fucking stupid her own self in her nose-candied days.

Probably.

19

PORTER WAS IN a real black-dog mood, toying with a tepid cup of tea in the canteen, when Wallace breezed in, full of hearty bonhomie, Porter hadn't been laid in like . . . six months . . . fuck.

He glared at Wallace, asked:

'What is it exactly you do, besides swanning around, getting loaded, swaggering as if you owned the place?'

Wallace gave what the literary writers call, when they want to slum, a shit-eating grin, asked:

'You wanna see what I do, get your ass in gear, buddy. I'll show you.'

Porter thought:

What the hell.

And said:

'I'm game.'

Wallace gave him a funny look, the one that read . . .

Aren't gays always, like . . . 'game'?

Outside, Wallace had a black BMW idling, and Porter whistled, asked:

Ammunition

'This your car?'

Wallace got in the driving seat, said:

'Pimp my ride.'

Try answering that.

Porter didn't.

Wallace said:

'We got us a suspect, linked to what appears to be another plot to bomb this fair city of yours.'

Porter asked:

'Shouldn't we have backup?'

Wallace was driving fast and with an ease that personified his confidence, the big car purring under his control. He sliced through a traffic snarl up, then pulled back his jacket, revealing what looked like a fucking Magnum in his belt. He said:

'I got you, buddy, right and this here little baby in my belt.'

Then he looked at Porter, asked:

'You ain't gonna punk out on me, bro?'

Before Porter could answer, Wallace said:

'I had you pegged for a get go kind of guy. Don't tell me I picked a putz, did I? You not up for this fellah, holler now and I'll let you out right now, you hear what I'm saying?'

It was hard not to as he was practically bellowing, Porter said:

'I'm in.'

Wallace gave a chuckle, one that came right up from his belly, said:

'Sweetest lines a guy can say, yeah?'

Porter wished he were carrying more than his wallet.

Never stand beside another officer while searching a crime scene. By separating, you present a smaller target and can view the scene from two different perspectives.
—The Law Enforcement Handbook

20

WALLACE PULLED INTO a street just off Clapham Common, a quiet residential street, and Porter thought:

Isn't it always so, the crazies find nice peaceful areas to reside.

And, he supposed, when you were wreaking havoc on the world, it was nice to have a decent home to return to after a busy day. You're blowing the be-Jaysus out of folk, probably good to get back, have a nice cup of tea, watch one of the soaps. He had to catch himself on, he was worse than Brant, already figuring the guy/woman/suspect was guilty.

Wallace said:

'Yo, earth to Nash, you coming or what?'

Porter asked:

'You want to fill me in a bit, give me some bloody clue to who we're . . . *interviewing*?'

Wallace laughed, said:

'You Brits, you sure talk funny, our guy is Shamar Olaf, how's that for a game of fucking soldiers. He was born plain old Joe Donnell but he got turned round, spent some time in Pakistan and the training camps in Libya. He's a doozy.'

Ammunition

Wallace was already getting out of the car, and Porter went:

'We do have evidence, I mean we're not just chancing our arm?'

Wallace closed the car door gently, said:

'Informant . . . god bless the treacherous bastards, plus, I got a nose for these things, this guy is the real deal.'

They approached the third house, it had a nice, tended garden, newly painted front, and the curtains were drawn. Wallace said: 'Follow my lead, you got that?'

He did.

Wallace produced a set of slim tools, and in a few seconds had the door opened and Porter suddenly grabbed Wallace's arm, whispered:

'We have a warrant right?'

Wallace said:

'Don't ever put a hand on me, and here's my warrant.'

He took out the Magnum, the gun actually looking quite small in his massive fist, he indicated the stairs and pointed Porter to the two rooms on the bottom floor. Wallace began to glide up the stairs, Porter, his heart in overdrive, opened the first door, expecting to be blasted at any second, wishing he had Brant for backup. It was the kitchen and empty. He wiped the sweat from his forehead and went to the next room, took a deep breath, opened that door, again, empty. It was a living room, wide-screen TV, and lots of books. Before he could let out his breath, he heard an almighty thud and rushed out to see a body come hurtling down the stairs, to land in a heap at the bottom. The man whimpered. He was clad in pyjamas, groaned, and tried to sit up. He looked to be in his late thirties, lean with an average face. Wallace was coming down the stairs, said:

'Meet Shamar, who has a bit of an attitude problem . . . that right, buddy?'

Wallace grabbed him by the hair, looked at Porter, asked:

'There a kitchen?'

Porter nodded and led the way, Wallace dragged the moaning man along, and in the kitchen, lifted him, plopped him in a chair, said:

'There you go. You had breakfast yet, Sha?'

He looked at Porter, said:

'The fuck you standing there for, Jesus H. Christ, brew some coffee.'

Porter had a real bad feeling and worse, he noticed that Wallace was wearing those surgical gloves . . . how'd that happen . . . and when . . . and where the fuck were his?

He made the coffee, instant, three mugs and asked the guy, who was coming round:

'How'd you take it?'

Wallace snorted, said:

'Any way he fucking gets it.'

And then he added:

'Black for me, two sugars.'

Porter put a mug in front of the suspect, found a bowl of sugar, some dodgy milk, and laid that alongside. The man looked at Porter for almost a full moment, and Porter didn't know if it was his imagination or just the whole unreal situation, but the guy's eyes, they frigging burned . . . with what? . . . zeal, idealogy, rage?

In one fluid movement, the guy swept the mug and stuff from the table, the milk slipping across the floor, the mug making a harsh noise against the bare tiles. Wallace didn't move, almost like he was expecting it, Porter had jumped, no point in denying it, and now the guy smiled, exposing yellow teeth. Wallace made slurping sounds with his caffeine, said:

'See what you're dealing with.'

The guy seemed to be gaining confidence by the minute and rounding on Wallace, said:

'American . . . the oppressors of the world. Killed any Muslims today?'

Wallace made a show of looking at his watch, a heavy metal tag, said:

'Ah, it's early yet, buddy, but we can get started.'

The guy said:

'I want a lawyer . . . now.'

Wallace moved right in close, asked:

'Where are the explosives, and when is the gig going down?'

The guy spit in his face.

Wallace didn't flinch, let the spittle run down his cheek, then slowly reached in his jacket, took out the Magnum, said:

'You have three minutes to tell me what I need to know.'

Porter tried to intervene, said:

'Maybe we should take this down to the station.'

Nobody answered him, and then Wallace shot the guy's ear off.

The explosion was deafening in the room, the guy howled in pain, grabbed at his ruined head, blood pouring down his neck, Wallace asked:

'You hear any better now?'

Porter cried:

'For the love of God, what are you doing . . . Jesus . . . come on?'

The guy managed to raise his head, pain etched in his face, and with a mighty effort he said:

'Go fuck yourself, you Yankee piece of shit.'

Wallace shot him in the face.

21

WALLACE WAS DRIVING fast and with a fixed determination, Porter was shocked, sitting in the bucket seat, like he'd been hit by a truck . . . or a Magnum.

Wallace asked:

'Where do you stand on pity fucks?'

Took Porter a moment to find his voice, then he said:

'I pity the poor fuck you just murdered?'

Wallace looked at him in amazement, asked:

'Hey, you're not gonna wimp out on me, bud, I didn't have you down for a pussy, is it some kind of gay thing? That what's going on with you, you on the rag?'

If Porter had been carrying, he was fairly sure he'd have shot him, he said:

'It's gay if you count being horrified by cold-blooded execution, how the hell do you expect to get away with it?'

Wallace laughed, said:

'You don't get it, do you, you poor sap. It's Homeland Security. I can do whatever the fuck I like, and what happened there, that was a message. . . . They want to sip with virgins, be bathed in milk, or whatever crap they believe, we're letting them know we're more than happy to send them on their goddamn way.'

Porter reached for his cigarettes. He'd nearly quit . . . well, down to five a day . . . five-ish . . . Menthol Lights. He fired one up and Wallace snapped:

'Yo, earth to pillow biter, did I say you could foul up my ride with that poison. It's like fucking manners to ask, and the answer would have been no.'

Porter took a long deep drag, let out the smoke in Wallace's direction, said:

'What you going to do, shoot me?'

They'd got back to the station, and Wallace asked:

'You gonna be pissed at me for long or you gonna lighten up, fellah?'

Porter tried to keep some trace of civility in his voice. He was British after all. Said:

'I'm going to be get pissed . . . not *gonna*, . . . g-o-i-n-g . . . and then I'll consider what action to take on your murderous act.'

He was out of the car and Wallace leaned out, near whispered:

'Well howdy-doody, thanks y'all for the lesson in that there grammar, and I tell you, pilgrim, you drop a dime on me, you is, as us rednecks say, . . . deep crittered.'

Porter spun back, asked:

'You threatening me, you. . . .'

He couldn't find a Brit-enough adjective to convey his rage and ended with 'wanker.'

Wallace laughed, burned rubber off the pavement.

Porter resolved he was going to be laid, if he had to buy a frigging rent boy, but as them Yanks said, *his ashes hauled,* he was gonna get.

That evening, he dressed for sex, tight dark jeans, a pair of boots that cut slightly into his left foot but pain was okay, kept you focused, ask Wallace.

He wore a crisp white shirt, open neck, no bling . . . come on, keep it simple, let his body do the talking, an ultra soft leather jacket, cream colour, and a splash of Calvin Klein. Good to go.

He had a very dry martini to set himself up and smoked one menthol, everything in moderation.

He didn't bring his car, let's not play silly buggers.

'Buggery' yes, silly . . . no.

He went to a club in Balham named, wait for it . . . O-ZONE . . . and worse, it had the logo . . . HITS THE SPOT.

Yeah.

But he'd been there before and it was a damn certainty to get off. He wasn't looking for a bloody relationship, he'd been there and had the scars to show. Nope, a few drinks, unwind, get fucked, go home. Two serious bouncers on the door, in the muscle T-shirts, looking like they'd escaped from Village People. He didn't know them, these guys changed as often as his underwear. He could flash, so to speak, his warrant card, breeze in.

From their exchanged look, they knew he was the heat, nodded at him, let him pass. Inside, he gave them the twenty-quid admission, got a smile from the drag queen taking the cash, and went in to the main bar/dance floor.

The basement was for S and M, Porter got enough of that in his job, and upstairs, well, that was private rooms for shagging. Porter prayed they wouldn't be playing Streisand, or worse, Garland.

Nope, some heavy hip-hop beat that wasn't the worst. He stepped up to the bar and a gorgeous guy, like a young Redford, smiled:

'And what would be your pleasure, sir.'

As Brant would say, thick as two short planks and stupid with it. Times were, he sure missed having that bigot around. He ordered a Campari and soda, stay mellow, and bought the guy a drink. The guy took a White Russian and when he got the look from Porter, lisped:

'Jeff Bridges in *The Big Lebowski*.'

Porter took his drink and took off.

Four minutes later, he scored.

Hey, you play, you gotta pay.
—Bonanno crime boss on hearing his wife had been
murdered after she dropped the dime on him

22

BRANT WAS SHAKING, not just his hands, his whole body. He was back in his home, a small house on the aptly named . . . Forl Road . . . as in forlorn. It had amused him once, not no more, he was dressed in a track suit, a navy blue London Met job. That normally tickled him as he'd nicked it from the Super. Sticking it to his boss had been among his favourite amusements

The painkillers they'd given him at the hospital weren't worth a shite, he said aloud:

'These aren't worth a shite.'

To the empty house.

The doctor had told him he was sure to experience post-traumatic stress disorder. Like it was fucking mandatory, and if he didn't, he'd be letting the side down. Yeah, well, bloody newsflash, he was feeling it, okay, happy now, you gobshites. And the rage—he'd always operated on a blend of anger, agitation, and aggressiveness—it was who he was.

Brant had been hurt before, knifed in the back by a couple of crazy kids who'd burned his dog . . . and what the fuck, as he thought of that damn animal, the dog that is. He felt a tear welling in his eye. Now he was seriously angry, to ride with the fear. Crying like a damned bitch.

Fuck no, no way.

After the knifing, he'd gone right back on the streets, meaner than ever and those two, the stabbing duo, they were dirt, literally, buried years ago and good fucking riddance. But this, this gut-twisting feeling, the sweat popping out on his brow, the tremors, Jesus.

Yeah, fine, he was of Irish descent, he knew the painkiller that never failed. Tore open his drinks cabinet, nigh splintering the wood, grabbed the bottle of Jameson, a twenty-five-year-old beauty he'd been saving, twisted the cap off as if he was twisting the neck of some bugger, got a lethal measure poured into a heavy Waterford tumbler, and drank deep, waited for the magic to light his belly.

He held the glass up to the light, sighed as the sun caught the intricate pattern. The odd time Brant had guests and, let's face it, not many called on Brant, unless to do serious damage. Porter, when he'd been unknowingly writing Brant's book. Brant had literally nicked the yarns and sold them as a book to a high-speed agent, and the damn thing was good to go, near ready to be published.

Fuck.

Porter had marvelled at the glass, commented:

'What a beautiful piece of real craft.'

Fags, they were into that fancy shite.

Brant, looking away, as if he were welling up, a near choke in his voice had said:

'Me old mum brought them over from the old country, t'was all the poor creature had to leave me when she passed.'

Truth to tell, the cunt had left him nothing but bitterness, and she spent no more money on crystal than she spent time on her son.

Porter was suitably impressed and relayed the moving story to Roberts at a later date. Roberts had laughed, said:

'He took them off a pimp he busted on the Railton Road.'

Porter had been raging, but what, confront Brant, yeah, right so he let it slide.

Brant was feeling better, picked up the phone, let it ring, then heard:

'Yeah?'

Tired voice, husky with cigs, bad booze, and worse men, He said:

'How you doing, Alanna?'

This was Lynn, a hooker who'd been around almost as long as Brant and they had history, a lot of it not so bad, he'd saved her arse more than once and ridden it a lot more. She said:

'I thought they shot you'

He laughed, genuinely amused, a rare occurrence for him. He laughed often but very rarely with conviction, he said:

'Just a flash wound.'

Like John Wayne, shrugging off massive bullet wounds.

Ammunition

Brant had watched *The Shootist* more times than he'd eaten late night kebabs in Piccadilly Circus. She asked:

'What'cha want, Sarge?'

Letting lots of the London hard leak over the question, let him know she was still a player, a tired one but hooking, you didn't expect to be energized. He said:

'A shag.'

She was silent and he could hear her lighter click, a gold Colibri he'd given her. She said:

'So, what else is new, give me twenty minutes. You're home I take it?'

'Home and horny.'

Click.

He wasn't horny, in fact, he never felt less like sex. The doctor had told him that gunshot victims often lost their usual appetites. He was fucked, pun intended, if he was going to let that be true. He took another wallop of the whisky, feeling better by the minute, and went upstairs, knelt down in his bedroom, and lifted up the carpet. He had a floor safe, got it opened, and took out his favourite piece.

The Sig Sauer, model 225. It had been revised to carry eight rounds of 9mm Parabellum ammo, he even had the grown-up version, the 226, which jacked fifteen rounds.

He thought:

Ammunition.

And aloud said:

'Yah little beauty.'

It was as close to affection as he got.

Lynn had said once:

'Little boys and their weapons.'

He'd of course, mounted her, muttering:

'Try this weapon.'

He could see Rodney Lewis in his mind, the big-shot city trader, smirking at him and Porter. Brother of a fucking rapist, and Brant was in, no doubt. He'd paid for the hit on him and would definitely try again.

That type always did.

Brant racked the Sig, said:

'Mr Lewis, you are dead fucking meat.'

He felt much better, must be the Jameson, worked every time.

He put the gun in his belt, walked, no, swaggered down to wait for Lynn.

The fear, nearly abated . . . nearly.

23

ROBERTS HAD SUMMONED Falls to his office. She'd been having a cup of tea and a blueberry muffin when she got the call. Lane, the cop who'd been on the Happy-Slapper arrest with her, had got up from his table when she'd entered. That was worrying. She wasn't sure he'd stand up, continue to maintain the lie about the set-up they'd pulled. Eyeing the muffin, she'd reassured herself:

'Naw, he's an old-style copper, he won't sell out the blue.'

Or black, in her case.

'Would he? . . . no, the fuckhead wouldn't have the balls.' He certainly wouldn't have the balls for long if he did.

She sighed. As if this weren't enough, she'd had another damn letter/card from Angie, the psychotic bitch.

Ammunition

Read:

Sweetie
Do you miss your little vixen? Don't you fret none, I'm com-
ing round real soon and then . . . you'll be coming . . . in a
flood . . . or a fall.

Xxxxxxxxx
Ang

Thing too, it kind of turned on Falls. Christ on a bike, how fucked up was she? The old urge for a line of coke surfaced and with ferocity, she could almost feel the icy drip down the back of her throat. Eat something sweet they'd told her in rehab when the compulsion arose.

Fucking words to live on.

She could eat Angie.

That's when the summons came, and she was relieved not to eat the muffin as her weight was definitely on the up.

Like her career, yeah?

She was a sergeant, wasn't she . . . muff that.

Andrews, the new gung-ho WPC, asked:

'Liz, you eating that?'

Liz? . . . the fuck did she come off?

Falls, without breaking stride, said:

'I'd skip it if I were you, I've noticed it goes right to your hips and . . . it's Sergeant to you, got that?'

She did.

And muttered under her breath:

'Cunt.'

Falls knocked lightly on Roberts's door, heard:

'It's fucking open.'

Good sign.

Roberts had a mess of files on his desk, a half-eaten slice of Danish, many many cups of tea? . . . and he looked like he was on the verge of a heart attack. He looked up, his eyes were bloodshot, and she thought:

Uh-oh, back on the sauce and big time.

He didn't offer her a chair, barked:

'This Happy Slapper, the photo gig, the mugging/mobile phone thing, how solid is that?'

She didn't hesitate, said:

'Rock.'

He gave her a long, cold look then asked:

'You sure on that, Sergeant? You want to change your mind about anything, this is the time. You'll lose yer stripes, but you'll save yer job?'

Jesus, she felt sweat on her neck, down her back, her thighs, thought:

That prick Lane.

Said:

'No, sir, we got him bang to rights.'

Roberts leaned back, let out a weary sigh, said:

'Lane, your colleague, says he didn't see it go down. In other words, he's bailing, so you're out on yer fucking tod, no backup, and I got to tell you, the press will be all over this. Last chance. Want to change your account, your report?'

She had to go with it. Said:

'I stick with my report, the arrest was white.'

Meaning, a good one, fuck, a great one.

Roberts was scratching his head, then ran his big meaty hand through his hair, now almost white and getting spares, said:

'McDonald is fucked. The witness on the old-age vigilante's screw-up has positively identified him. It will be released in a few hours.'

Falls actually felt for McDonald, asked:

'Isn't there anything we can do. He'll do jail time for this?'

Roberts seemed almost sad, no one liked to see the blue go down, he said:

'Naw, he's done and you get to tell him, give him time to get a lawyer, tell him get a real expensive one. He's going to need the best.'

Falls was panicked. If they could throw McDonald down the shitter, what about her? She attempted:

'Wouldn't it be better, sir, if he heard it from you, you know, his commanding officer and all?'

Roberts had already dismissed her, was opening a file, said:

'Never could stand the bollix.'

Falls went to the pub, she ordered a large Stoli, no fucking ice, thank you very much, and defintely no fucking conversation. She gulped it down, ordered another, and the barman did consider a query but saw her expression, said:

'Yes ma'am.'

'Ma'am?'

She nearly laughed but the small death she was feeling prevented it. She went to the back of the bar, got out her mobile, and with a sinking heart, called McDonald.

I've got to die sometime so I may as well go this way.
—Crime boss Angelo de Carlo en route
to prison at the age of sixty-seven

24

McDONALD FELT LIKE shite warmed over. He'd come to at the foot of his bed, still in his clothes.

Sort of.

His jeans were round his ankles, and he vaguely remembered bringing some babe home and . . . oh, Jesus, buying dodgy chicken from some street vendor, muttered:

'Memo to dumb-arse self, NEVER . . . like never, buy stuff from these guys, and Christ, never eat the crap.'

Judging by the pool of congealed vomit, near his head, he'd eaten it . . . some anyway, as he spotted some green-looking meat with thin bones near the door, unless he'd offed the woman.

The way he was acting these days, fuck, anything was possible. He pulled his jeans off and then had to throw up, still on the floor, said:

'Nice . . . real class, wouldn't Mum be proud now.'

He crawled on his belly to the press near the bed, ripped open the door, and thank fuck, the silver wrap was still there.

He managed to organize a line, spilling white powder like dandruff, due to his shaking hands, and got a line or four done, if badly, kept saying:

'So spill freely, we can inhale that later, just get the bastard thing into your system.' Maybe being still half drunk helped, but the coke hit quick and the ice down his neck was a sign of better things to come. He lay on his back with a sigh of relief, vomit still on his chin, did he care?

Like fuck.

Shouted weakly:

'I love nose candy.'

And he did.

Whether it loved him was a whole other metaphysical gig he wasn't prepared to go into.

Ten minutes later, he did a few more, keep the am, lines of communication open, he was laughing intermittently now, knew it couldn't be a healthy sign. AND AS COKE DIC-TATES, SOMETHING MAD, he went into his living room, which looked like the wreck of the *Hesperus,* rooted under some seat covers, and grabbed his newest possession.

A Makarov 9mm automatic, he'd bought it for what . . . ninety quid, from a Russkie he'd been drinking with, in some dive off the Railton Road. Ivan had told him it was the pre-ferred weapon of the Eastern bloc agents.

Yada, yada, what the fuck ever, but did it work?

He'd meant to test it on the whore but kept getting wasted and forgetting.

The coke hit another level, of almost euphoria, and he said:

'Happiness is a warm gun.'

Fucking Beatles, yeah. Even ol' Paul had his troubles, the wife having legged it.

Did he have any Beatles shit?

The phone rang, and he nearly shot himself in the foot, barely got his finger away from the release.

Picked up, it was Falls, and it flashed across his fevered brain, get her over, give her one, and then she told him:

He forgot all about the Beatles.

He was fucked, more so that McCartney and like bollocks, he never got to have a wife who could leg it.

Tears were running down his face. They were going to arrest him.

Him.

Once, the brightest star in the Met.

The Super had said so.

David Grey, on his album, had whined:

Something about where'd it all go wrong?

Ah, sweet Jesus.

He pleaded:

'Falls, Liz, yeah, it's Liz, right . . . what should I do, what can I do?'

He wanted her to save him, was that so damn hard?

There was a pause, and then she said:

'Run'

He thought it must be the dope, he had music references

Ammunition

littered all over his head. Wasn't 'Run,' the title of that Snow Patrol song?

Falls gulping the dregs of her double had the mobile slightly down from her ear, but she still heard the sound of the shot.

She would hear it for the rest of her life.

25

AS FALLS STORMED into the station, the cops got one look at her enraged expression and got out of her way.

Real fast.

Andrews, still smarting about the weight quip, got in her path and was literally shouldered aside.

The desk sergeant, never a Falls groupie, whispered:

'On the rag, eh.'

If she'd heard that, he'd have eaten it.

Count on it

But perhaps there is karma, some kind of cosmic balance, as later that evening, watching his beloved Liverpool beat the shite outta Newcastle United, his telly blew up.

Go figure.

Falls didn't knock on Roberts's door, just barged in and before he could mutter:

'What the . . .'

She launched.

'Well, Chief Inspector, I made the call, as you *ordered,* to McDonald, remember . . . he's a cop.'

Ammunition

She paused, was that . . . is a cop or . . . was?

Roberts feigned indifference, his face showing, *shit happens,* he asked:

'He want any help from you?'

She gave a smile, if a blend of rage and murderous intent can produce such, said:

'I told him to run.'

Roberts gave a nasty chuckle and Falls wondered how she'd ever liked this prick. He said:

'He'd be wise to take it.'

She had to physically rein herself in, a wave of bile rose in her gut, and she said, spinning on her heel:

'Be a tad difficult with a fucking bullet in his skull.'

And she stormed out, slamming the door with all her might, hailed a cab, said to the driver:

'Take me to The Clapham Arms.'

He wasn't all that sure where it was, but something told him not to ask. He'd figure it out.

There were NO SMOKING decals all over the taxi and as she put a cig between her lips, he ventured:

'Wanna light?'

Little fanfare the exit make
Unheralded
is the lone departure

26

THESE LINES, FROM a little-known Irish poet, might well best describe McDonald's exit from London.

The brass were quick to shut down the whole story, and a new terrorist alert kept the focus off some poor schmuck eating his gun.

Favours were called in, threats made, and the whole sorry episode was allowed to simper, slouch away.

McDonald's parents were told he was killed in a tragic accident, and they couldn't afford to come down to London so the Met had him cremated and sent him by second-class mail from Paddington.

His mother put the urn over the fireplace, right beside a photo of Charles and Diana, no one had yet told her that Charles was married again, the odd visitor was a little startled to be told, that's my boy there, on the mantelpiece.

Brant, on hearing the news, said:

'Silly bugger.'

Roberts felt a daily sense of guilt.

Porter wished he'd known him better.

Falls, Falls went on a massive bender and midway through this, she was in a pub in Balham.

Balham?

Don't ask.

It was a bender.

She'd hit that lucky third vodka where the hangover has abated and you're even considering a touch of grub, considering, not actually going to eat.

A woman appeared, a young man in tow, said:

'Hey, sweetie, might we join you?'

Angie.

The vixen.

And the young guy, Jesus, the bloke she'd framed for the Happy-Slapper gig. She was truly lost for words.

Angie was dressed to fuck, black leather mini, black boots, and a blouse that bore testament to the miracle of the Wonderbra.

Angie sat, said to the guy:

'Be a dear, get some drinks in, and oh, a large vodka for our favourite policewoman.'

Falls rallied.

'The fuck do you want, you crazy bitch?'

Angie laughed, nothing she liked better than warfare, she said:

'To see you, darling. I get hot just remembering our love-making.'

And Falls felt her face burn. Must be the damn booze,

does that to you. Before she could utter a scathing reply, Angie said:

'The young dreamboat with me, you know him, of course, I was hoping we might work out something, make this whole silly charge . . . how should I put it . . . evaporate?'

Falls took a deep swallow of her almost neat vodka, then:

'Never happen. He's going down and with any luck, you'll be joining him.'

The guy was back, carrying a tray of drinks. He looked at Falls with pure hatred, plonked her drink down so it spilt, sat down, Angie cooed:

'Liz, sugar, you remember John . . . John Coleman, the poor lamb you set up or do you set up so many you forget their names. He sure won't forget yours.'

She squeezed his thigh, his eyes never left Falls, Angie continued:

'We have a proposition for you, love. You drop this non-sense against John, and I won't sell my night of torrid sex with black, recently promoted sergeant. Does that sound . . . reasonable?'

Falls was fucked, knew it, reacted by taking on the stare of Coleman, leaned over to him, said:

'Keep looking at me like that and I'll take your fucking sheep's eyes out.'

He pulled back, way back.

Angie was thrilled.

'See, John, didn't I tell you she was a downright tigress?'

Ammunition

Angie raised her glass, asked:

'So, let's toast our deal, what do you say, Liz, cherry pip?'

Falls threw her vodka in her face, stood up, said to the guy:

'You ever give me a fucking look again, I'll cut your balls off.'

And she stormed off.

Angie, in a warm tone, shouted:

'See you at your place soon. Drinks on me, darling.'

Outside, Falls had to stand against the wall for a moment, try to get a grip on her world that was spiralling so far down the toilet, she didn't even know if it was worth flushing. A homeless guy approached, asked in a concerned tone:

'You okay, missus?'

'Missus'?

She nearly laughed but was afraid if she started, she might never stop. She linked his arm, asked:

'How about I buy you a big drink, mate, how would that be?'

He concurred it would be just dandy.

They were halfway down the street when he tried to put his hand up her skirt, and with almost reluctance, she broke his nose.

The Glock, chambered in 9mm, is capable of placing five-shot groups inside a 2.5-inch circle at a range of 25 yards

27

PORTER NASH WAS sitting at home, and yeah, his place was immaculate, spotless in fact.

A gay thing?

No, he just hated dirt.

He was listening to Mozart, not that he'd be sharing that taste with the blokes at the station . . . they'd fucking love that.

Ask him.

'Don't you like to listen to Barbra Streisand?'

Right and still had his copy of 'YMCA.'

Thing is, they'd buy it

He'd bought six bottles of that fine Belgian ale Duvel.

It sure tasted marvellous.

He needed some escape as his mind was a whirl of conflict, the nagging guilt over the death of the man at Wallace's hand, the suicide of McDonald, Brant being shot and worse, what Brant would do in retaliation, it would definitely be biblical . . . and soon.

Too, his diabetes was raging unchecked, his glucose levels through the roof, and hey, who'd time to get it seen to.

Drinking . . . was that smart . . . take a wild frigging guess.

Reason it tasted so good and even . . . wicked.

The sex in the gay club had been a wondrous release, despite the guy asking him if he loved the New York Dolls?

Name one single by them, go on, dare you.

He'd nearly said that, but he was up to his groin in the guys arse, so it hadn't seemed the time for a pop quiz.

He smiled.

The guy had come in a torrent and then asked:

'Wanna do some E?'

His doorbell rang. The only caller he ever got was Brant, and he was kind of relieved. It would be good to get that lunatic to take on Wallace.

Wasn't Brant.

Wallace.

All bonhomie, good cheer, etc. He held out a bottle of wine, said:

'Peace?'

Porter didn't move, snapped:

'How'd you know where I live?'

Wallace gave that shit-eating grin, good ol boy, the gee shucks shite he did so well, said:

'Bro, I'm in counterterror. I know where everybody lives, so do I get to come in?'

Reluctantly, Porter stood aside, nodded:

Wallace strode by, walking in as if he were the owner, but

every inch the cop, his eyes checking exits, scanning the room, he set the bottle on the coffee table, said:

'Wanna grab us some glasses. I don't think we should drink it by the neck, and I bet you got real fine wine glasses.'

Wallace pulled off his duster, a long black one naturally, eased his huge frame into a chair, plonked his cowboy boots on the table, said:

'This here is comfy, bit faggy but what the hell, man's home is his castle, fairy or otherwise.'

Porter went to get some glasses and half wished they weren't Waterford crystal, a tin cup would be more Wallace's speed. He was arranging cheese spread on crackers and thought:

The hell am I doing, playing right into his stereotype?

He binned the crackers.

When he returned to the front room, Wallace was smoking a thin cigar, and a Glock sat on the table. Porter wondered if Wallace intended to kill him? He set the glasses and the wine bottle down carefully, asked:

'What's with the gun?'

Wallace was drinking one of the Belgian beers, smacking his lips in appreciation, said:

'That brew has a bite, now see that there Glock, most folk, they figure it's all plastic, but it's only 17 per cent that, the barrel and the insides, they are solid steel, go on pick it up, see if I'm right?'

Not the hell sure what was going on, Porter picked it up,

marvelled at how light it was, turned it over in his palms, and Wallace asked:

'Wanna take a pop at me, Port?'

Porter put it down, opened another beer, sat down, and got ready for whatever it was was coming down the pike. Suddenly, Wallace was all motion, up, his hands holding a hankerchief and he almost reverently wrapped the gun in it, put it in his duster, went:

'Ah.'

Porter had a real sinking feeling, asked:

'What's happening here?'

Wallace drained the beer, belched, asked:

'Got any snacks, pretzels, chips, like that?'

Porter ignored that, waited:

Wallace sighed, said:

'Insurance, ol' buddy, you see, you're that rare kind of cop, don't get me wrong, I respect it, but times, they are a-changing and thing is, I figure you might rat me out on that raghead whose ticket we punched. You can't help it, you have morals and me, well, I got yer prints all over this here weapon, a certain scumbag gets offed, guess who's in the frame. You keep your mouth shut, let me protect democracy, and hey, no problemo. You sure you don't got any like, nuts or stuff, don't faggots always have little dainty snacks and shit?'

Porter was on his feet, wondering if he could take him, get the Glock, and Wallace smiled, no warmth, the real hardarse showing, without moving a muscle, he said:

'Forget it, bro, you wouldn't get past the coffee table.'

Then he drained the beer, chucked the bottle on the carpet, said:

'You pillow biters like to have crap to clean up, am I right?'

He flicked the stub of the cigar across the room, stood, said:

'Hate to threaten and run but the enemy never sleeps. You free Friday night, I found me a club does line dancing, and serves ribs, have us a hoedown. Y'all take care now, hear.'

And he was gone.

He was right on one point, Porter was down on his knees, sweeping up the debris of the visit.

28

BRANT HAD HAD him a fine ride, had rolled off Lynn, slapped 'er on the arse, said:

'You sure know what it's for, girl.'

Lynn had made all the appropriate noises of delight as he'd gone at it, and she knew, Brant of all the men on the planet knew it was a crock but he didn't, to coin a phase, give a fuck. He'd gone to the fridge, got some cold Heinkens, handed her one, and she chided:

'No glass?'

He liked her, she had a lot of spunk, and it was one of the few qualities Brant appreciated, he said:

'Fucksakes, you'll want paying next?'

In all their time, he'd never actually given her cash for the deed, but in a hundred ways he'd paid her through other means. Having a lethal weapon like him in your corner . . . priceless.

Anxiety was still in his gut so he rifled through Lynn's handbag, not even a moment's hesitation. He wanted something, he went for it, and hookers, they always had some tranks.

Ammunition

Bingo, a sheet of Valium, he took two, 5mg, knocked them back with the beer. Would have killed for a pint of Guinness, he'd been to Galway once, and man, it was a work of art to watch them build a pint, get that creamy head, and all the time, giving you lots of friendly chat.

Way to live.

As he waited for the pills to crank, he knew, knew the only cure for the gut wrenching was to take out Rodney Lewis. The guy was definitely going to take another run at him, and if Brant wasn't real careful, the bastard might get lucky. You didn't get to be a rich bollix like him by being stupid. Thing was, he wasted the fucker now, they'd come right after him. Who else had motive.

He was letting the problem sit when the doorbell went. He had on a white robe he'd nicked from the hospital. It was warm and smelt of comfort, it had two big pockets, and he had the gun in the right one, gripped the butt, opened the door.

A seriously dishevelled Falls stood there, pleaded:

'Could I get some coffee?'

Jesus, he'd seen her in some states, especially in the days when she'd been living on the nose candy but now, she looked like she'd been sleeping rough, he asked

'What, you think this is bloody Starbucks?'

Then headed back inside, said:

'Shut the door, there's a draught.'

She did, came in, stood, looking like a lost cat. He made a cup of instant, added a generous dollop of his fine Jameson, handed it to her, lit a smoke, and gave her that too.

Her body was trembling, she gulped the coffee, asked:

'Is there something in this?'

He smiled, said:

'Yeah . . . hope.'

She began to feel a bit better, Brant was the most unpredictable person she'd ever met, and yet, you were knee-deep in shite, he was the guy who would find you a shovel. You'd probably have to do the digging, but he'd keep you company. She said:

'I broke a wino's nose.'

He laughed, said:

'Jaysus girl, they have it bad enough, you have to go round kicking the fuck out of them as well?'

She drained the coffee, said:

'God, that was good.'

And then . . . the silence, Brant would wait forever when he knew you wanted something, and she as sure as hell wanted something.

Help.

She tried to buy some time, said:

'I feel so bad about McDonald.'

Brant sat opposite her, those stone eyes holding her, reading her, and he asked:

Ammunition

'Why?'

Anyone else in the world, they'd go the pseudo-route, mutter sympathetic stuff, like:

'There was nothing you could do, there was nothing anyone could do.'

But Brant, no bullshit, right to the core.

She faltered, then:

'I feel I should have helped, you know . . . ?'

And he smiled, that awful smile that said:

'Sure.'

He stretched, and she wondered if he was hurting from the shooting but ask . . . ask Brant . . . *sure.*

He said:

'He was a cowardly fuck, he took the easy way out, and how many times . . . did he fuck you over, or have you forgotten the Clapham Rapist, McDonald as yer backup?'

She was stunned. All those years he'd never once referred to how he'd saved her life. Before she could even think of a reply, he continued, he said:

'Reason I mention our rapist mate is he has a brother and, guess what, he's the fuck had me shot. Funny old world . . . isn't it?'

She had to know, went:

'What are you going to do?'

He stood, said:

'I'm going to get you another of those kick-arse coffees, and then you're going to tell me what you want?'

He did and she did.

Told it all, the set-up of the Happy Slapper, Lane selling her out, and the reappearance of Angie.

His face lit up at the mention of the Vixen and he interrupted:

'Well fuck me sideways, that's great, I always felt that was unfinished biz.'

Then Lynn strolled in, wearing one of Brant's shirts, her ample bosom spilling out. She nodded at Falls, not in an unfriendly way but more a kind of total disinterest, and for some reason, that irritated the bejesus out of Falls, like . . . *hooker, dissing her?*

Brant turned to Lynn, said:

'Take off, babe, this is work.'

Lynn gave Falls another look, one that said:

'I've had him . . . what's your gig?'

Then, oh so casual, leaned over, kissed Brant on the lips, said:

'Catch you later, honey.'

He slapped her on the arse, said:

'Long as that's all I catch.'

And . . . winked at Falls.

Not for the first time, she wondered what the fuck had happened to her once bright vision of police work, some skewered notion of righting wrongs, doing the best you could, and all that good Oprah crap.

Part of her began to envy McDonald being out of the

whole sorry game, and Brant, waiting till Lynn had gone, swung back to face her, said:

'Ammunition.'

She was lost, said:

'I'm lost.'

He near sang:

'But now you're found . . . ammo, baby. It's all we need . . . or, of course . . . , love.'

Then, very carefully, he told her how it was going to go down.

Did it scare her?

Did it fuck?

It's easier to run than explain.

—Clyde Barrow

29

RODNEY LEWIS WAS home, a nice log fire going, so, it was artificial, it looked the biz. And being in the financial game, he knew appearances were all. He was wearing a smoking jacket, he didn't actually smoke but you get the drift. It had the monogram, *R,* on the pocket, in gold stitching. He was real proud of that:

Class.

Who said you couldn't buy it.

Fucking Labour government is who.

They were going to get theirs, and big time, in the next election, and with the Tories back, let the good times roll. He was sipping from a snifter of brandy, a fifty-year-old cognac, and the aroma, . . . bliss. He'd had a lobster dinner at his private club and a rather delicious crème caramel to follow. He let out a contented belch, thought:

Life is sweet.

Except . . .

Brant . . .

The continuing problem.

Ammunition

He'd decided to let it sit for a while, just do . . . nothing and wait for inspiration to hit. It always did, why he'd made so much cash in the city. Meanwhile, he had the satisfaction of knowing the bastard had to be hurting from the gunshots. And better, knowing that Rodney was coming, Brant would be on constant alert and then, out of nowhere, when he let his guard down . . . bingo, he'd be hit.

Rodney wasn't going to farm out this contract, nope, not after the last fiasco. He'd do the piece of garbage himself.

He replayed the scene in his car with the guy who'd messed up the deal, and the rush of the adrenaline when he'd shot the poor dumb idiot. And that's how he'd do Brant, up close and personal. He owed it to his late brother to keep it in the family, and he really wanted to have that rush again. The look on the victim's face when you shoved the shooter in his mug.

Shooter?

He laughed aloud, like something out of *The Sweeney*.

He was still chuckling when he felt the cold barrel in the nape of his neck and he dropped the snifter, the cognac staining his Harrods pyjamas, those suckers had cost, like a bundle. He knew it was Brant, he heard the intake of breath and knew from recent experience it was the moment before the squeeze, and he tried:

'Sergeant Brant, is this really the smart thing. They'll know it's you, I mean, let's talk this through.'

He was pleased with his calm tone, the matter-of-fact

voice he assumed, and then he had a brilliant idea. He knew precisely what to say to stop the maniac.

The first shot went right through, exiting his left eye and the second, a little lower, lodged in the bone of his nose. Rodney and his brilliant idea slumped forward in the chair, blood adding to the already ruined silk pyjamas.

The smell of cordite nearly wiped the aroma of cognac, but with fifty-year-old stuff, it's hard to quite erase that kind of quality.

The killer used a small Swiss army knife to dislodge the bullet from the bookcase, he considered rooting around in Rodney's face, retrieving that one. he was whistling "Dixie" as he contemplated his work, then thought the hell with the second bullet. Did he really want to get in the guy's face?

He was still smiling at his pun as he let himself out.

30

JOHN COLEMAN, THE Happy Slapper, still couldn't quite
believe the turns and twists his life had taken over the past
few weeks. He'd been walking along, his mind preoccupied
by minor irritations. Oh God, what he wouldn't give to have
them back.

Then fuck, like hell opened up and Armageddon hit him.

The lady cop, scratch that, the bitch cop, had appeared out
of nowhere, literally jumping on him and claiming he'd been
one of those wankers who slapped people and then photographed it to send to their friends. Next thing, he was being
charged and looked like he'd be doing jail time.

For what?

Then, just as he had abandoned all hope, an unlikely sav-
iour appeared, Angie, a blond stunner who said she'd fix
everything and mainly . . . *fix* the cops. Turned out, she had
history with Falls, the bitch cop, and even better, had lever-
age. Plus, well, sort of, he got to fuck Angie a lot. Now he
wasn't stupid, he knew there was something off about Angie,

she had this cold look sometimes, put freaking shivers down your spine but what . . .

Like he had a choice?

He was along for the ride . . . till . . .

Till, as Angie said, Falls withdrew the charges. Oh yeah, Angie banging on about how they'd make a mint on suing the police for false arrest, harassment, undue emotional trauma, and a whole slew of other stuff.

Yeah, right.

Soon as Falls relented, he was so out of all this, bye bye Angie. And man, was he ever going to keep a low profile from then on. He was sitting in the kitchen of his tiny flat, drinking tea, and longing for the day when all this crap was done. Angie would be by later, and he wished he could work up some energy for that. First, she'd want bed, then the mad schemes would begin. His doorbell rang and he sighed, she was here earlier than he'd anticipated. Maybe he'd say he'd a headache.

Like that would work.

Opened the door to a tall man, dressed in a very expensive suit, and . . . get this, with a huge smile. Coleman let all his frustration leak over his voice, asking:

'I know you?'

Let a little hard dribble in there too, so the guy would know, this was not the day to be fucking with him. The guy's smile widened and he said:

'No, but you're going to.'

With that, he punched Coleman in the gut, hard, and pushed him back into the flat, closed the door, Coleman was doubled up and the guy looked at him, walloped him twice across the face, said:

'That's to get the smirk off you.'

The man strode on in, asking:

'Where's the kettle, I'd kill for a cuppa?'

Coleman managed to mutter:

'I'm going to call the police.'

The man, without even looking back, said:

'I am the police.'

He'd found the kettle, was plugging it in, asked:

'Get you something or you good?'

Coleman chanced a glance at the door and the man said:

'Bad idea, I'd have to break one of your legs and you wouldn't like that, oh no, not one bit. Do you have any bread, a cuppa is not the same without a nice slice of toast.'

By the time the man had fixed his tea and toast, and settled himself into an armchair, Coleman had recovered enough to walk in, stand by the table, keeping that between him and this . . . lunatic.

The man, midbite, said:

'You know the song, clowns to the left of me, clowns to the right of me?'

The fuck was he on about?

Before Coleman could reply, if there was one to this, the man said:

Ammunition

'Well, sonny, in your case, it's cops, all over your unlucky arse.'

He reached in his pocket, and Coleman was convinced he was going to shoot him.

Instead he pulled out an envelope, slapped it on the table, said:

'Your going-away money.'

Coleman, hating himself, echoed in an almost childish voice:

'I'm going away?'

The man smiled, delighted, said:

'See, you catch on fast. You take a nice six-month vacation, get away from all this lousy weather, and when you come back it will all be over. You can go back to your shitty, boring life.'

The contempt in the man's voice gave Coleman a false sense of courage, and he snapped:

'What if I don't?'

The man wiped some crumbs off his suit, said:

'Don't you hate when that happens?'

Then he abruptly stood up, said:

'If you don't, forty kinds of hell will descend on you.'

As he headed for the door, he suddenly turned and Coleman instinctively ducked. The man laughed, asked:

'How much time do you think you'd serve for the stash under your mattress?'

Coleman was confused, further, asked:

'You mean like . . . heroin?'

The man had the door open, said:

'No, I mean, under your mattress.'

Coleman followed him out into the corridor, in spite of himself, went:

'I don't do that stuff.'

'Bet you a fiver you'll look, though. Gotta run, good people out there needing our protection. Don't bother writing, you just kick back, relax.'

When Coleman went back inside, he was trembling and his stomach hurt. He swore he wouldn't look under the mattress.

That lasted for tops, four minutes, he pulled the blankets, tore the mattress off, no heroin but a single sheet of paper, that read:

Had you going . . .

31

FALLS WAS DRINKING, seriously. She'd sworn so many times she'd keep a lid on it, rein it in.

Yada yada.

I mean, c'mon, the whole Happy-Snapper gig, threatening her whole career, that snake Lane, not backing her up, and McDonald eating his gun.

Fuck.

Who wouldn't drink?

And then, having to go to Brant . . . again . . . and making the pact with the devil. When she'd asked:

'What are you going to do about the Happy Snapper?'

He'd given a satanic smile and asked:

'You really want to know?'

Guess not.

As she'd been leaving, he said:

'Think . . . biblical.'

That was the whole point, she didn't want to . . . think, at all. Thus, the vodka, Stoli went down like a prayer, albeit a brief one. It was nine in the evening, she was dressed in her

Ammunition

old Snoopy nightshirt, it was old and comfortable, she was on her second . . . third? drink, with a mixer of bitter lemon, low cal, of course, like that made a fat bit of difference. Bitter it certainly was. Tupac was on the speakers, with 'Thugs Get Lonely Too.'

Christ, that sang to her.

The doorbell went and she figured . . . Brant, with results, she gulped another swig, get in gear for . . . whatever.

Opened the door to Angie.

Dressed to kill?

Short black leather skirt, black tight T-shirt, black tights, with a sheen, or was it the vodka? And a suede jacket over her shoulders. She was carrying a bag, said:

'Goodies.'

Falls felt such an overwhelming hatred for the cow. Here she was again, fucking with Falls's life, bringing chaos and destruction and with that knowing smirk. She looked mock hurt, asked:

'Aren't you going to ask me in?'

Falls stepped aside. At least the guy wasn't with her, what was his name . . . Coleman, yeah.

Angie literally skipped in, looked round, said:

'Oh dear, sweetie, we haven't been doing much cleaning, have we?'

She began to unload the bag, bottles of vodka, snacks, and what looked like a packet of weed . . . to a cop.

She said:

204

Ken Bruen

'I'll get the glasses, shall I, though I see you've already got a jump start.'

Falls felt an icy calm descend on her, and she decided, this was going to end. One way or another. This bitch was out of her life. She watched as Angie bounced around, full of that malignant confidence, the total control she was accustomed to exerting.

She poured herself a large glass, settled herself on the sofa, letting lots of thigh show, and asked:

'See anything you like, lover?'

The last time she'd been round, they'd ended up in the sack, to Falls's never-ending regret and shame. Angie raised her glass, said:

'To the future, ours, right hon?'

Falls raised her glass, took a lethal wallop, asked:

'What do you want?'

Angie smiled, she had great teeth, and then went:

'Opps.'

Wiping the lip gloss off the rim of the glass, she said:

'You might want to wipe some of this gloss yourself, would you like that?'

And Falls, to her horror, did want to, so badly. She had to physically bite down, get a grip, and she let her voice stay cold, repeated:

'What do you want?'

Angie's face went through the brief change, the mask slipping for a moment, to show the dark demon that lived there.

Ammunition

Falls actually backed up a step, the fleeting glimpse of who, or what, Angie was had raised goosebumps on her arms. She put out her hand to steady herself, and it curled round the bottle of Stoli, which had been left on the bookcase, holding the bottle for comfort. Angie let her eyes linger on Falls for a moment then turned away, said:

'My new little friend has disappeared, now I wonder why. I'd plans for that boy and I have a sneaky suspicion that you, Liz, mind if I call you that, I think you had something to do with it.'

Falls felt a rush of emotions, delight that the bastard was gone, she was off the hook, fear as to what Brant had done to him, and mostly, dread of what Angie had in mind. Angie crossed her legs, letting the sound of nylon hover, then said:

'Liz, unless I get him back, I'm going to have to go to the papers with our . . . affair. You think the *Tabloid* would be interested in that?'

Falls lashed out with the bottle, catching Angie square across the top of her head, then screamed:

'Don't fucking threaten me, you piece of crap. I'm a fucking police officer.'

Vodka packs more of a wallop than you'd expect.
—Sergeant Elizabeth Falls

32

ANGIE WASN'T MOVING, she was sprawled on the sofa, her eyes rolled back in her head.

Falls dropped the bottle, moved to the sofa, tried:

'Angie, Angie, you okay?'

Nope.

Falls, panicked, felt for a pulse.

None.

She staggered back and nearly slipped on the Stoli. She grabbed it, pulled off the cap, and drank from the neck, the liquid running down her Snoopy shirt. She let the booze burn her stomach then gasped:

'I've fucking killed the bitch . . . oh Jesus.'

Calling Brant was out of the question, and she certainly wasn't calling the squad.

Fuck, no way.

She had to get the body out of here and now.

She grabbed her car keys, pulled Angie upright, got an arm under her shoulder, and pulled her to the door, she opened it cautiously, no one around and did Angie have a car, no, no sign. She got her in the her own backseat, then slid behind the wheel and started driving, very carefully.

As carefully as you can when you've whacked someone's lights out and guzzled most of a bottle of spirits. She didn't know how long she was driving, her mind refusing to come up with a plan. Finally, she stopped, in Croydon, beside a deserted warehouse. Turned her engine off.

She checked her surroundings, not a soul and better, beside the warehouse was a Dumpster. She got Angie out and dragged her by the hair to the Dumpster, Angie's shoes were gone.

Where were the fucking shoes, in the car?

She got the lid off the Dumpster, that sucker was heavy, then with an almighty effort, pulled Angie up, threw her in the garbage. The smell from the thing was appalling, a blend of decaying vegetables, she hoped they were vegetables and urine with . . . curry?

She slammed the lid down. It made a ferocious bang, and she muttered:

'Nice, real fucking nice, wake the freaking dead.'

And she began to giggle, said:

'Angie, didn't wake you, did I?'

Hysteria engulfed her, and she added:

'Don't ever fucking call me Liz.'

Then a blast of cold wind hit, and she stopped, realized she had to get the hell out of there.

She did.

When she finally got back to her flat, she looked in the backseat for Angie's shoes. They were there. She took them into her home and first thing, she had a large shot of the Stoli, then a few more and later, tried Angie's shoes on, they fit:

Snugly.

She was still wearing them when she passed out, thinking:

The night wasn't a total bust.

She'd been meaning to buy new shoes.

Who had the time?

33

BRANT WAS DOZING when the phone shrilled. He grabbed at the receiver, mumbled:

'Yeah?'

Heard:

'Congratulations, big boy.'

Very posh tone.

Only one person called him that and, of course, the haughty flighty accent. It had to be that mad cow, his agent, Linda Gillingham-Bowl

Fucking name. Take you a week to get it out.

And he shuddered, he'd ridden the cow, Jesus wept. He'd managed to con Porter Nash into writing most of his novel and then got hold of this agent, a real high-profile one, but fuck, old. He'd meant to ply her with drink, trick her into giving him an advance, and . . . instead, he'd given her one.

Real bad move.

But it sure made her work like a banshee on his book. He needed coffee, lots of it.

Ammunition

But here was:

'It's wonderful you got shot.'

He sat up, his eyes groggy, said:

'I'm glad you're pleased.'

He heard her give that artificial laugh they practiced in agent school, and she said: 'You are so droll, you naughty boy, of course I'm relieved you're alright but with the imminent publication of *Calibre,* it's perfect. Hero cop shot on eve of publication. It's such wondrous PR'

He hated the bitch, said:

'Glad I could have helped.'

She was highly excited, said:

'Everybody wants you, all the major chat shows, and with that rugged charm and roguish humour, you're a natural.'

'Jesus.'

Before he could add more, there was a pounding on the door, he said:

'Don't go away, I have to answer the door.'

More of that awful laughter as she said:

'I'm hanging on for dear life, you devil.'

He pulled the door open and cops piled in, led by Porter Nash, a slightly ashamed-looking Nash, who said:

'Sergeant Brant, I'm here to arrest on you suspicion of the murder of Rodney Lewis.'

Brant, took a moment, then said:

'Can I just finish my call?'

Indicating the phone.

Porter asked:

'Your lawyer?'

Brant laughed, said:

'Fuck no, better, it's me agent.'

He picked up the phone, said:

'Gotta go, babe. I've been arrested.'

She was near orgasmic in her delight, said:

'You sweetheart, you're such a marketing dream, this is ideal, you want me to do anything?'

'Yeah, put up bail.'

He put the phone down, turned to Porter, asked:

'Can I get some coffee?'

Porter produced a warrant, said:

'This allows us to make a search of your premises and yes, while we're conducting the search, you may make coffee, I'm afraid I'll have to accompany you.'

Brant smiled, asked:

'Got a fag?'

Any other place being searched would have been tossed with total disregard, the cops not giving a shit about what they damaged or ruined:

But Brant.

Uh-uh.

He might be under arrest, but he was far from gone and they knew better than to fuck with his stuff, so when they found various items of dope, porn, they ignored it, Brant had a long memory. Their brief was to find a Glock, and that's all they searched for, if not too diligently.

Brant was savouring his coffee, drawing hard on the menthol cig Porter had given him. Porter was staring at him, asked:

'You don't seem too worried. This is a serious charge, and everybody knows you threatened him.'

Brant smiled, no warmth or humour, his most calculated one, said:

'You know Porter, you were with me, so if everybody knows, you told them, I thought we were mates?'

Porter felt terrible, they were mates, if the most unlikely pairing on the planet, but Porter took his role as cop very seriously, said:

'If you took the law into your own hands, you're no longer a policeman.'

Brant was still smiling, asked:

'When was he hit?'

Porter, taken by surprise, needed a moment to think, then told Brant the time and date.

Brant dropped the cig on the floor, ground it out. Porter had to fight the impulse to clean up. Brant said:

'I've an alibi.'

Porter knew all about Brant's circle of hookers, who'd do anything for him, said:

'Your hooker crew won't bail you on this one I'm afraid.'

Brant stared right into Porter's eyes, said:

'Oh, it's not a hooker, much much better.'

Porter had to know, asked:

'Might I know who it is?'

Brant took his sweet time, then:

'Falls, that's Sergeant Falls to you.'

Then he stuck out his hands, asked:

'Wanna cuff me?'

Porter had considered it, anything to wipe that fucking smile off his face, but said:

'No, I don't think that will be necessary.'

Brant sighed, said:

'Pity, I thought you gays, you were into all that S and M stuff.'

The lead search cop looked in, said:

'We found nothing, sir.'

Porter was barely holding it in, snapped:

'Nothing?'

'No, sir.'

Brant looked at the cop, winked.

The press had a field day with Brant's arrest, the killing of Rodney Lewis smacked of vigilante cop justice, and they'd been keen to nail Brant for years.

His agent, true to her word, had a high-priced lawyer arrive, and without definite evidence, Brant was bailed. Roberts had been despatched to get over to Falls's place, see if the alibi held up.

The Super wanted Brant to go down, shouted at Roberts:

'You tell that black cunt to be very careful about helping Brant get out of this. If he goes down, she's going with him.'

Roberts wisely, said nothing.

On the steps of the police station, Brant gave an impromptu press conference, replied to all questions:

'Read it in my new book, *Calibre*, due next week.'

His agent was over the moon.

The man was a publishing bonanza.

34

FALLS WAS IN a deep stupor when Roberts came banging on her door. Took her a moment to come round, then she felt her stomach heave, a biblical headache kick in, the banging was ferocious on the door, she screamed:

'Jesus, give me a bloody minute.'

And heard:

'It's the police. In a minute we'll force the door.'

Roberts was alone but in no mood for Falls and her nonsense. Falls thought:

Oh, God. They've found Angie already. I'm fucked.

She opened the door, saw Roberts, and nearly threw up on him, he pushed her aside, said:

'On the piss again, that's a help.'

She closed the door quietly, the world spun for a moment, and she had to struggle for balance. Roberts surveyed the wreck of the room, bottles everywhere, and then took a closer look at Falls, said:

'I like the shoes, very classy, though I'm not sure they go with the T-shirt.'

Ammunition

Falls gazed in horror at Angie's shoes, how the hell did that happen, and at Snoopy on her shirt. Like her own self, he was the worse for wear. Roberts picked up a bottle of Stoli, examined the top, asked:

'What'd you do, crack someone over the head with this?'

Before Falls could utter a word, he poured a healthy measure into a mug, said:

'You better have some of this, hair of the dog that bit you. But I think the dog was rabid from the state of you here.'

And he offered the mug, she could hardly hold it from the shakes, but managed to get it to her lips, drank greedily. The liquid hit her like acid and she gasped, thought she was going to spew wholesale, Roberts watched with a certain detached interest. He'd been down this road himself so he wasn't entirely unsympathetic. It was, in fact, Falls who'd hauled him back from the toilet so there was a certain symmetry in this. The battle in her stomach waged for nearly three minutes. Doesn't seem long, but if you're the one with the stomach, it's eternity:

Her stomach won out and the booze settled in for another session, waiting for more of the same. Roberts said:

'Sit down before you collapse.'

She did, sit that is.

Kicked off the shoes, Christ, soon as she was able. She was burning those fuckers.

Roberts made some coffee and as he did so, Falls recalled bits and horrendous pieces of the evening before.

Holy shit, she'd killed the Vixen.

Roberts put a steaming mug before her, said:

'No more booze. Get that down you and let me see if I can get any sense out of you?'

She managed to speak, said:

'I'm okay now. Why are you here?'

Roberts sat back, remembered when Falls had been the wet dream of the nick, and gung ho, believing a black WPC could really make a difference. The years had soured her beyond belief, but then he didn't believe a whole lot in anything either. Truth was, he'd always liked her and so he went easier than he'd planned, said:

'I'm going to give you a break, for old times' sake, I could start asking you where you were with on a certain night, and more importantly, who you were with?'

Falls was convinced it was Angie. She was going to go down for the psycho bitch, but in truth, she didn't feel any remorse for walloping her . . . killing her? . . . well?

Roberts said:

'Rodney Lewis was murdered and, of course, the most likely suspect is our man Brant.'

Then he did her the favour, told her the day and time of Lewis's demise, and asked:

'Sergeant Falls, were you with Sergeant Brant on the day and time in question?'

Falls had no idea. She couldn't for the life of her remember anything beyond the hazy events of the previous evening. She said, without hesitation:

Ammunition

'Yes, sir, I was.'

They both knew she was lying, and it hung there for a moment, blackening whatever affection, bond, had been between them. Roberts sighed, said:

'Be very sure you want to do this . . . Liz.'

She nearly laughed, the last person to use her first name was rotting in a Dumpster.

Fuck, maybe she'd kill anyone who came by, sure would give the postman a turn.

She reached for the bottle, and Roberts looked like he might protest, but then he waved her on. She hefted the bottle in her hand, looked at Roberts, and realized how easy it would be just to go on a wild murderous spree, as long as you had booze to lubricate the process, how hard could it be?

She poured a smallish amount, took a sip, and sat back, let out a tiny sigh of, if not contentment then a certain resignation. Roberts was half tempted to join her. He hated like hell to see a good copper go down the shitter. He said:

'You go to bat for Brant, you're more or less washed up, not that you seem the brightest prospect just at the minute, but the Super, you know he wants Brant and if you're the one to save him, then, you're the one he'll destroy.'

She nodded:

Roberts stood up, asked:

'You really want to jettison your career for . . . Brant?'

She smiled. It was such a rare event that Roberts was momentarily taken aback. He'd forgotten how pretty she could

222

be and his damn fool heart skipped a beat, the smile was tinged with such sadness that he wanted to put his arms round her, tell her it would be alright.

Yeah . . . sure.

They were coppers and, worse, English ones, such a gesture would have scared the bejesus out of them both.

She stood too, and seemed like she might shake his hand, she asked:

'You think I have a choice?'

And Roberts, who knew Brant better than most anyone, which wasn't a whole lot, said:

'I'll do my best for you.'

She reached out, touched his arm, said:

'You always have.'

At the door, he said:

'Go easy on that stuff, we need the best and brightest.'

She gave another of those killer smiles, said:

'Not to mention the blackest.'

Then she closed the door. Roberts hesitated for a moment, debated going back in but moved to his car, he thought about her last remark, and trying for the cynicism he needed to survive, he whispered:

'Hang on to that sense of humour, you're going to fucking need it.'

The best ammunition is the stuff you keep in reserve.
—*Sergeant Brant*

35

FALLS'S ALIBI LED to the case against Brant being dropped.

His agent threw a huge party in Covent Garden, and Brant invited everyone, including his hookers. As the party progressed, they'd do major biz, everybody wins. Falls was a no-show.

Porter showed up, looking sheepish and approached Brant, who was opening yet another magnum of Champers. Porter put out his hand, said:

'No hard feelings.'

Brant stared at him, said:

''Course not, but will I forget you arrested me? Like fuck.'

And he moved away, carried on a swirl of goodwill from his followers. Porter got a gin and tonic, slim-line tonic, sat in a corner, said he'd down that then get the hell out of there, heard:

'Yo buddy, how's it hanging?'

Wallace, looking more like a cowboy than ever, fringed buckskin jacket and, of course, the boots. He sat down beside Porter, took a large swig of his bourbon, said:

'All's well that ends well.'

Porter stared at him and Wallace laughed, said:

'You really need to lighten up, bro.'

Before Porter could reply, Wallace said:

'I told you before, you've a conscience and that's a dangerous commodity in these dark times. If you're thinking of, you
know, blowing the whistle on our other . . . event, lemme just
run something by you.'

Porter waited:

Wallace was studying his boots, as if they fascinated him.
Said, in a stone voice:

'Suppose the cops were to search another cop's home and
they found a Glock, a Glock with your prints on it and gee,
guess what, it was the gun offed the Lewis dude. Would it be
stretching it to believe you did the deed as a favour for your
buddy Brant?'

Porter was stunned, asked:

'You're blackmailing me?'

Wallace stood up, punched Porter on the shoulder, said:

'Just running a little scenario by you, bro. Y'all take care
now, gonna see if I can score me a little Brit chick?'

And he was gone.

Porter swept the gin and tonic off the table, said, in a near
perfect imitation of Brant:

'Bollocks.'

36

FALLS, IN A feeble attempt to tidy up, had taken a brush to sweep the floor and found Angie's handbag under the sofa. She opened it, found the usual stuff and a tiny automatic. She got a fresh bottle of vodka, seal intact, and sat it on the table. She eased herself down, the automatic in her hand, you racked it, and bingo, a round ready to go. She looked at the vodka, unopened, said:

'Virgin like.'

And gave the tiny smile that had so entranced Roberts.

She held the tiny gun up to her mouth, tasted it, cold.

And wondered what McDonald had thought of in his last moments, she regretted not washing the Snoopy T-shirt. She'd have regretted all the rest, but it was too much . . . ammunition?

37

CRACK OF DAWN in Croydon, a wino was rooting around in a Dumpster, the smell didn't bother him, he out-odoured it easily.

He was reaching for what looked like a box of Kentucky Fried Chicken. He sure liked the Colonel's recipe, and fried? Accessorised his brain.

A hand shot up, a voice going:

'What's a girl gotta do to get a drink round here?'